Palace Hill Comprehensive School
boasts two very special pupils —
the royal princes William and Harry.
Read the intimate details of life at
Palace Hill in this compelling story . . .

Which prince will win the heart of the
delectable Peanut?
What happens at Nick Knuckle's dreaded
initiation ceremonies?
Will the two First Years ever find their classroom?
When will these boring questions end?

All this and much, much more will be revealed in
the thrilling saga of PALACE HILL!

ACKNOWLEDGEMENTS:

I would like to thank Bob Hescott, who wrote a sizeable proportion of **"PALACE HILL — Your Mother Wouldn't Like It"**, on which this book is based. In fact he wrote a lot of the best bits. In particular I'd like to thank him for inventing Blatherwick, and for being brave enough to go to the Ju-Ju zone, alone, without an 'I-Spy' compass, or even leather trousers.

PALACE HILL — the book,
is based on the original television scripts
by Peter Corey and Bob Hescott.

Photographs reproduced by kind permission of
Central Independent Televison plc.

by Peter Corey

Based on the Central Television Series
PALACE HILL — Your Mother Wouldn't Like It

Hippo Books
Scholastic Publications Limited
London

Scholastic Publications Ltd.,
10 Earlham Street, London WC2H 9RX, UK

Scholastic Inc.,
730 Broadway, New York, NY 10003, USA

Scholastic Tab Publications Ltd.,
123 Newkirk Road, Richmond Hill,
Ontario L4C 3G5, Canada

Ashton Scholastic Pty. Ltd.,
P O Box 579, Gosford, New South Wales,
Australia

Ashton Scholastic Ltd.,
165 Marua Road, Panmure, Auckland 6,
New Zealand

First published by
Scholastic Publications Limited, 1988

ISBN 0 590 76076 9

Made and printed by Cox and Wyman Ltd.,
Reading, Berks.

Typeset in Times by COLLAGE (Design in Print),
Longfield Hill, Kent.

For Joel, Hannah and James

1

NEW BEGINNINGS

"We have nothing to fear but fear itself." Do you know who said that? I mean apart from me just then, or apart from you just now if you're reading aloud. Don't know? Give in? Well, it was Franklin Delano Roosevelt, who was President of the United States of America four times. Mind you, he'd never met Nick Knuckle. If he had done, he might have said, "We have nothing to fear but fear itself and Nick Knuckle." Or he might have kept his mouth shut if he knew what was good for him, which he did, because you don't become President of the United States four times unless you really know your onions. You don't even become a greengrocer *once*, unless you really know your onions.

There is no such thing as a typical Monday, and today was no exception. It was the first day of the new term at Palace Hill Comprehensive School, the school attended by the Royal Princes

William and Harry. The school also attended by the much feared Nick Knuckle, and the school *not* attended by Franklin Delano Roosevelt, who was: (A) American, and (B) Dead.

You see, although the school had extended its catchment area to include overseas pupils, it had so far drawn the line at offering places to dead United States presidents, particularly ones who went around talking about fear.

The school had, however, offered places to the two eleven-year-olds who now stood trembling at its Forbidding Gates. Well, Broken Gates really, rather than Forbidding. I mean, casual passers-by were not often heard to say, "Cor! Look at those Forbidding Gates, Norman." They were far more likely to be heard to say, "Cor! Those gates could do with a lick of paint." Nonetheless, it was not with Paintpot and Brush that the two pupils now stood at the gates. Oh, no. It was with Fear and Trepidation — hardly the tools of your average decorator.

A casual glance would have revealed that they were dressed from head to foot in brand new Palace Hill uniforms, the finest that "H JAMTON, Schools and Military Outfitters (NOW BY ROYAL APPOINTMENT)" could supply. Closer inspection would also have revealed that every item of clothing was clearly marked (as per school instructions) with embroidered name tapes, lovingly sewn in the night before, by their respective Doting Mothers. There they stood, scrubbed, starched and shaking, for what seemed like days. It was, in fact, just long enough for you to turn the page . . .

"Come on," said the girl, who was the slightly braver of the two. "We can't stand here all day!"

"Why not?" reasoned the boy, with the kind of logic that you'd expect from someone who came from a long line of cowards. In fact, his grandfather had served in the army, and had always been the first to volunteer to run away.

"You will stand and fight with the rest of us!" his Commanding Officer would shout.

"Do you mind if I sit and fight? I could do it very efficiently from behind this large sheet of Totally Bullet-Proof Metal."

"No! Get out there and die for your country! And don't come back here until you've done it."

"He was only annoyed because he hadn't thought of it first", the soldier was later to tell his grandson.

Back in modern times, and at the school gates, the girl was following her own logic, which told her that Fear of the Known was every bit as bad as Fear of the Unknown. Common sense told her that if the bell went they would get into trouble, and she immediately passed this thought on to her friend.

"We'll get into trouble anyway if we go in there," replied the boy, pointing beyond the fierce-looking gates. "I'm too young to die."

"Why? How old do you have to be?"

"No! You don't understand!" The boy was becoming agitated. "Terrible things can happen to you in there! You know my mate Kelvin's brother?"

"Yeah . . . what happened to him?"

"Nothing. He didn't go to this school. But a pal

of his did. And they pulled his head off and stuck it up his nose!"

"That's stupid!" countered the girl, who wasn't as daft as she looked. "How could he breathe?"

"I don't know, do I?" snapped the boy, who *was* as daft as he looked. "I'm just telling you what happened! And . . . " He paused, to achieve the maximum effect:

"They make you sing."

It worked. The girl was mortified.

"S-sing? W-what do they make you s-sing?"

"I'm a Little Teapot."

The words and tune to "I'm a Little Teapot" were not the girl's strong point. In fact, they were definitely her weak point. Now, if she'd been asked to sing something by Wet Wet Wet, she could have sung it backwards. Her father believed that Wet Wet Wet was already doing that, and delighted in telling her so. Of course, you couldn't blame him. He belonged to a different musical era, when the hit songs of the day were being written by people who were now drawing their pensions, and being sung by Cliff Richard. But it's part of a parent's job to poke fun at the way their offspring dress and behave, if only because *their* parents did it to *them*.

The Two Newcomers stood there.

Their years at primary school had been formative ones, and had sent them into the Big World armed with a multitude of useful skills, such as Reading, Writing, Adding, Subtracting, Forward-Rolling-with-Dress-Tucked-Into-Knickers (girls), Forward-Rolling-without-Dress-Tucked-Into-Knickers (boys). The girl had

4

also learned Ballet, and Piano to Grade 5. The boy had learned Fighting and Playing the Recorder to the Grade just above "Making-the-Dog-Howl" and just below "Really-Annoying-the-Neighbours". (I think it's the Grade called "Giving the Teacher A Nervous Breakdown"). But neither of them has learned "I'm a Little Teapot", not realizing that one day it would come in handy (unlike Reading and Writing, which, for them, would turn out to be of no use at all). They were struggling with the problem of what to do, when the school bell sounded, signalling, to these two new First Years, the start of their Six Years' Hard Labour, without any time off for good behaviour.

THE SCHOOL

At first glance Palace Hill Comprehensive School looked like a very large Public Lavatory. No one ever gave it a second glance (except people looking for the toilet), but if they had done it would still have looked lavatorial (it was probably the writing on the walls that did it).

There were various rumours that the school was actually made of crispbread and balsa-wood, but these rumours were without foundation, as was the school. It was falling down, but much slower than expected. Nonetheless, the pupils were discouraged from whispering in its corridors, just in case the sound-waves caused the building to collapse totally. So, there it sat like a crumbling relative.

It was exactly the sort of building that Prince Charles condemned in long speeches. Which made it all the more ironic that his two sons were its star pupils. But more of them later.

"Hello."

The Talking Blancmange that now smiled its cakey smile into the startled eyes of the two First Years was Doughnut, the Fat Boy who Everybody Likes.

"Hello."

This second voice belonged to Mandy, the Safe and Boring Friend.

The Two First Years braced themselves for the torture and humiliation that was about to follow. But none came. In fact, Doughnut and Mandy seemed *friendly*. There must be some mistake. They must have come to the wrong school.

"This *is* Palace Hill, isn't it?" asked the girl.

"Er, yes." Thinking had never been Doughnut's strong point (he usually brought a note from home to get himself excused from it), and so he did have to check by pulling the badge off his blazer pocket and getting Mandy to read it for him. As their conversation continued it became obvious that:

Yes — Doughnut and Mandy were friendly.

No — they didn't want to pull anyone's head off and stick it up their nose.

No — they certainly didn't want to hear anyone singing "I'm a Little Teapot".

But — Doughnut could murder an Eccles Cake if either of them had one hidden about their person. They hadn't, and they also declined Doughnut's offer to search them just in case there was one hidden away that they didn't know about.

However . . . Mandy had a warning for them: "Nick Knuckle may want to show you the

Blue Dolphin, if he catches you."

"Yeah, but you'll be OK," reassured Doughnut, "if you stay away from the lavs."

"Yes," agreed Mandy, "don't go near the lavs."

"We won't," confirmed the girl, and the two First Years set off in search of their classroom, a search which was to take them to many strange places . . .

PRINCES AND PUPILS

One of the places that the search did not take them to was the school noticeboard. This was a pity, because, apart from containing a more than adequate map of the school, it also had, standing in front of it, the Two Royal Princes.

William and Harry were now old hands at the ways of the comprehensive system, and were currently engaged in writing down their timetables from the master copy on the noticeboard. Time was when they would have had a servant to complete the task for them. But school regulations had been tightened, and servants in school were no longer allowed. William could see the good sense in this. After all, there were pretty well a thousand pupils at the school, and if everyone had just a basic skeleton staff of, say, twenty servants, that would mean . . . erm . . . he would make a note to get his Adding-Up Servant to calculate the answer on his Personal Computer when he got home that evening. But it certainly sounded like it would be a *lot*.

William had always found it odd that none of the other pupils ever discussed their servants. He also found that he had mixed feelings about returning to school this term. The holidays had been such fun. There had been the usual trip to Balmoral, where they had been greatly amused by the Royal Corgis keeping the local wet fish merchant trapped up an oak tree for six days and nights. His situation was made worse by the fact that the overpowering smell of fish had attracted thirty-seven local cats into the tree with him, which naturally increased the enthusiasm of the dogs. Things came to a head when he was joined by four squirrels and a badger, none of which had any taste for fish, and even less sense of smell. This in turn caused the local gamekeeper to organize an impromptu shoot, much to the alarm of the fishmonger, who was very anti blood-sports, and was getting anti-er by the minute, particularly since he had become a prime target. The situation was only resolved when the corgis, who are not stupid animals (despite appearances), decided that the local postman's bottom was much nearer to the ground and to their teeth.

So, if you are wondering why you never got a reply to the letter that you sent Her Majesty this summer, describing your holidays and asking her if she could do anything about your hamster's boil, the chances are that your original letter is now inside a corgi, along with bits of postman.

The highlight of William's summer holidays, however, was Carrying Money. His father felt that it was time a Member of the Royal Family should attempt this strange ritual. After all, Common People did it all the time, and it didn't seem to have any really lasting ill-effects on them (although it did seem to make them speak badly, but William could always stop doing it at the first sign of a dropped "H"). Well, this had proved a great delight, from the jangling noise it made as one walked along, to the way it shone as one held it up to the sun. After a while it did tend to make the linings of one's pocket rather grubby, but this was a minor problem, and was soon solved by having a Money-Polishing Servant following William everywhere, and occasionally giving William's money a quick "spit and polish", with the careful application of a square of the finest Flemish Silk, and good honest elbow-grease. As the experiment was such an unqualified success, William's father promised that next year he could have a shot at Spending Money.

Harry's summer holidays had been equally eventful. He had found True Love. Not that it had been lost. It had been there all the time. He just hadn't recognized it. Oh yes, he had expressed an interest in this young girl before, but only really because William also . . . what was the expression? Harry had heard some of the other chaps using it. Fancied her. That was it. Only because William also fancied her. What was that? Peer-group pressure? Sibling rivalry? Bloody-mindedness, grandfather would say. But, in the words of Shakespeare, Harry had "played

11

the game of love, and won". Or, in the words of his uncle, he had "pulled a cracker". Harry's uncle had often used this expression in connection with finding a new girlfriend. But Harry didn't understand it at all. He had pulled many crackers, every Christmas in fact, but had never found a girl in any of them. Perhaps things were different in the navy.

The object of Harry's affections was Nick Knuckle's kid sister, Peanut. The only person he had not confided in was his elder brother, and rival in love, William. Harry realized that he must tell his brother, and before too long. In fact, perhaps now would be as good a time as any. It will obviously be difficult, so let's leave them to it . . .

Another place that the First Years did not visit was an area known as The Bins. No one really knew how this area had got it's name, although it was where the bins were kept, which may well have had something to do with it. Had they come here, they would have witnessed, and almost certainly have taken part in, a ritual that had become as much a part of the first day of term at Palace Hill as had the new teachers fighting over a parking space. It was Peanut Knuckle cementing a Second Year into the school wall. Not usually a thing that happened to Second Years, but this was a rather small and First Yeary-looking Second Year, so Peanut could be forgiven for the mistake.

"There," remarked Peanut, putting the finishing touches to her handiwork. "And think yourself lucky that I didn't make you sing 'I'm a Little Teapot'."

"Yes, Miss. Thank you very much, Miss."

"See . . . the . . . dog." The voice came from the other end of the metal studded dog lead held in Peanut's free hand.

"Eh?" said the Peanut end.

"See . . . the . . . ball," said the other end.

"What's he on about?" Peanut end again.

"The . . . dog . . . is . . . eating . . . the . . . ball," said the other end.

"I'm teaching him to read." This time the voice came from neither end of the lead, but from the mouth of Mandy. Gosh! Had Mandy become Peanut's Safe and Boring Friend? No. She had simply attached herself to Peanut in the hope of being near Harry, for whom she still carried a very large torch (though what Harry would do with a very large torch was anyone's guess). In order to avoid talking to Peanut, for whom she did not carry a torch, or even a dead match, Mandy was teaching Yob to read. Yob was situated on the other end of the studded lead.

"What for?" That was Peanut, speaking with her cynical view of the value of education.

"The . . . Yob . . . is . . . eating . . . the . . . book." That was Yob, speaking with his mouth full.

"Come on. Let's go and find some First Years and show them the Blue Dolphin."

Two of the First Years that Peanut would not be finding (or showing the Blue Dolphin to) were our Two Newcomers. In fact, no one would be finding them for a while, as they were well and truly lost . . .

One place they did not visit on their journey to complete lostness was the video room. Had they done so, they would possibly still be there, and not lost. They would possibly have witnessed the arrival of Quiff, sidekick to the Great Nick Knuckle, carrying his History Project. They would probably have seen his surprise at seeing the room was not empty. They would almost certainly have shared his confusion at meeting PC. They would definitely have shared his total lack of comprehension of anything she said.

PC was one of the overseas pupils that Palace Hill had recently opened its catchment area and its doors to. Originally from America, where she had attended Degrassisass High (as an elephant's eye), PC was a real Computer Buff. And this was the problem. Quiff wasn't.

"Hi. I'm PC. What's your identifier?"

"My what?" Do you see the problem?

"Your identifier." Then in Plain English: "Your name, you Flip-Flop!" (Well, more or less!)

"Oh, I see. Er . . . Quiff."

"What's this?" enquired PC, noticing the video under Quiff's arm.

"Oh . . . it's my History Project. I'm doing a Project. On History. And this is it. Part of it."

Like all Americans, PC had a deep interest in all things historical. This has something to do with the fact that Americans have such a short history themselves, that they covet other people's. This usually causes them to spend thousands of dollars travelling the world, staying in over-priced hotels, and taking millions of photographs of each other. PC was no exception.

"Wow! Mega-flop! And I suppose you want me to breadboard it for you? Well, I've got a bit of downtime, so we could give it a benchmark. Is this your grandfather? If you like I can dump it, and you can keep it in your hopper. OK? Right! Let's bootstrap!"

Quiff often had trouble with simple things like "Hello", and "How are you?". He was now wishing that he had never started this conversation. He was not, however, wishing that he had never started his History Project. He had learned so much. For instance, he now knew that:

There is no proper name for the back of the knee.

Adolf Hitler was a terrible juggler.

The Man from Delmonte is not called William of Orange.

The Plimsole Line is not what sailors put their shoes in when they go to bed.

"Why are you doing this History Project?" asked PC, loading the video cassette."

"Well, my dad says that if I don't do better at school, I've got to get rid of my pet."

"Oh. What have you got?"

"A flock of sheep."

And they settled down to watch the video.

Long ago . . . in Ancient Rome . . . of course, it wasn't called Ancient Rome then because it was quite new. It was probably called New Roma, or Rome New Town, something like that. Anyway, Rome had seven hills, and the only one that still exists today is Jimmy Hill.

The Emperor of all the Romans, or Caesar for short, was Julius Caesar. He had the same name as his job. They did that in those days. I mean, the baker was called Mr Baker, the butcher was called Mr Butcher, and the traffic warden was called all sorts of nasty names. The Welsh still carry on this ancient tradition. Only they do it slightly differently. For instance: the baker would be called Evans the Bread, the butcher would be called Jones the Meat, and the traffic warden would be called Clamp the Wheel.

There's lots of things we've got now that they didn't have then. For example they didn't have television, videos, space invaders, cars, British Rail, McDonalds, Bros, Alf, and they only had a very few Cliff Richard records. But they did have the Games, where people could go and watch men killing each other, or being attacked by wild animals. We still have that today — it's called football. But, after a while the Games got boring. I mean, if you've seen one lion with indigestion, you've seen them all. So Caesar said to his Entertainments manager, "I'm bored. What can I play now?"

"Conkers."

"That's a good idea! I'll go and 'Conker' the Britons!"

And so he did. Caesar and his fleet set sail in 56BC and arrived in Britain in 55BC. They were sailing backwards. As soon as he landed, he said those famous words, "Vini, Vidi, Vici", which is Roman for "Wine, Women, and Pop Videos". But he soon found himself surrounded by Britons, covered from head to foot, and all points east and west, in blue paint.

"Why are you from head to foot in blue paint covered?", enquired Caesar in Schoolboy English.

"Ita isa nota bluea painta, you wally," replied the Briton, in Football-Hooligan Italian, "It's wode, innit John!"

"Julius," corrected Julius, and wished he hadn't. "But why are you wearing wode?"

"We have to wear wode today, don't we? Because it's Wodensday." (Wednesday to you and me.)

"But aren't you cold?"

"Freezing, Squire. But that's OK. Because, tomorrow, we get to wear our animal skins."

"Why? What day is it tomorrow?"

"Fursday."

Well, the Romans set about improving Britain. They added "cester" to the end of several place-names to make them sound more . . . er . . . different. They also built lots of motorways. The first one they built was the M1, which they didn't do very well, and it's still being repaired to this day. You can't blame the soldiers, they were fighters, not labourers. And, anyway, the pay was very bad. They weren't even paid peanuts, only salt!

With Caesar away from Rome, things went from bad to worse. The Roman peasants were revolting. They stopped going to the Roman Baths, and refused to pay their rent. This was because they believed that Governor Nero was on the fiddle. Soon they were many weeks behind with their rent, and many of the landlords went bust (you can still see some of these busts in museums). One of the landlords, Mark Anthony (I don't know his surname) was so short of cash that he tried to borrow some money from the peasants who were witholding their rent. He called a meeting, and appealed to them, saying, "Friends, Romans, Countrymen: Lend me your arrears."

Caesar eventually returned to Rome, where he was given a hero's welcome. Several of his pals slapped him on the back. Unfortunately they were all carrying their daggers at the time (well, they had to carry their daggers as there were no pockets in their togas). Caesar received fatal injuries, from which he never recovered. He was succeeded by Augustus, who was a Leo.

"Wow! That's a mega-flop!" enthused PC, as the video came to an end.

"Oh. I thought it was quite good."

"No! You Pico-Cruncher! You're not patched to my thread, are you? 'Mega-flop' means brilliant!"

"Does it?" said Quiff, suspiciously. He was sure that he'd never understand anything she said.

William had a different problem. He would never understand the ways of the heart. Harry's revelation about Peanut had hit him like a bombshell, whatever that felt like. Royals don't normally show their feelings, but here he was, blubbing like a Real Person.

"One really must pull oneself together," he told himself. "One's supposed to have a stiff upper lip, but instead one's got a soggy lower leg. One's ruined ones shoes, and shrunk ones tie. No girl is worth that!"

"Hi there, Heir!"

William was jolted out of his self-pitying reverie by the voice of Madeline, the Captain of Sport. A girl for whom the word "failure" did not exist, she entered and won every sport event in existence: high jump, low jump, long jump, short jump, swimming, shooting, running, vaulting, hockey, soccer, rugger, tennis, netball, football, softball and handball. Her cupboards were covered in cups, and her drawers were full of medals.

"Why so down-hearted, regal chum? You look like a wet weekend!"

"Well, it's rather personal . . ." began William.

"Say not another word, royal personage. Fifty press-ups, the answer to everything!" So saying, she hurled herself at the ground, the vibrations from which threw William off balance, and brought him down beside her.

Needless to say, none of this was observed by our two First Years, who were still rather lost.

Rumblings of a different kind were taking place elsewhere.

"*Are we in this flippin book or not?*"

"*I don't know.*"

Huddled in a small huddle were the Rest of the School . . . all three of them.

"*Cus, I mean, if we're not going to be in it, we might as well go home, mightn't we?*" reasoned one.

"*Yeah, but what if we go, and then we're in it? We won't be, will we, cus we won't be here, will we?*" reasoned a second.

"*Er . . .* " reasoned a third, bringing the discussion to a different intellectual level.

"*Yeah, but if we hang on just in case, and then we're not, we're going to feel right wallies, aren't we?*" Number One pursued their line of argument.

"*Er . . .* " Number Three struggled with theirs.

"*Tell you what,*" compromised Number Two. "*We could stay here for a bit, see what happens. Then, if we're not in the book, we can go home. Yeah?*"

"*OK. Yeah.*"

"*Er.*"

And so they stayed, unnoticed by anyone, especially the two First Years, whose journey had not yet taken them past this particular corner.

So where had their journey taken them? Well,

more or less everywhere, other than anywhere that they wanted to go. The directions given them by Doughnut had seemed confusing, but, since he had been at the school for some time, they naturally assumed that he knew his way around. This was their first mistake. Their second mistake was possibly taking a wrong turning.

School uniform is not ideal wear for jungle travel. If they had known that Doughnut's directions were going to take them deep into the heart of Tarzan Country, they would have brought along a change of underwear.

"Perhaps we should have turned left at the bins," mused the boy, who was beginning to feel like Crocodile Dundee.

It is apparently not possible to circumnavigate the globe on foot, that is without getting your socks wet. The two First Years were therefore very surprised to discover, some time later, that that was precisely what they had done. And what adventures they had had!

What adventures *had* they had?

Well, too numerous to list here, and definitely enough to win you a wall-full of Duke of Edinburgh Awards, if not a place on "Operation Raleigh" (but not enough for a place on *Bob Says Opportunity Knocks*, I'm afraid).

The pyramids are in Egypt. I mention that in case any of you were away from school when they did Geography. It was in Egypt that the boy was able to exercise his knowledge of Speaking to Foreigners, picked up on a family holiday to Benidorm.

Perhaps this would be a good place to pass on

some tips, which you may find useful as you jet around the world. Here's how to make yourself understood when travelling abroad:

In Italy: Simply add "A" to the end of every word. But don't forget the arm waving, as this is very important.

In Spain: Add "O" to the end of as many words as possible. Arm waving will also help here.

In France: Here you should add "Le" to the beginning of as many words as possible. Also try clearing your throat in the middle of words. Arm waving is less important, but an onion in one hand and a poodle in the other could get you off to a flying start.

In Germany: Put "Ze" in front of as many words as possible, and also throw in the odd "Der" now and then. Don't wave your arms about, but carry a big sausage.

In Belgium: As in France and Germany, but also carry a bag of chips.

In Greece/Turkey: Pepper your conversation with "Innit?" Arm waving is very important, unless you're dancing.

In Scandinavia: Sing everything you say, and wear a blond wig.

In Poland/Czechoslovakia/Russia: Keep your mouth shut and wear a disguise.

A useful phrase to practise: "Gosh! How on earth did you guess that I was English?"
HAPPY TRAVELLING!

The two First Years' journey finally brought them, tired and travel-worn, to outside the school lavs, the one place that they had been told *not* to go. The boy, however, was in no state to heed the warning . . .

"But you know what Mandy said," pleaded the girl. "If you go into the lavs, Nick Knuckle will show us the Blue Dolphin!"

"I don't care what he shows us," countered the boy, a note of desperation in his voice, "I've got to go!" And so saying, he went.

The girl stood outside for a few minutes, expecting either screams and yells, or the safe return of her friend. She got neither.

"Oh, well . . . better make sure he's OK." And she entered the lavs . . .

4

THE BLUE DOLPHIN

"GOTCHA!" yelled Nick Knuckle, who had read too many *Sun* headlines. The girl struggled, both with her captor, and with what to say as a suitable reply. She finally settled for "Agh!", which seemed as apt as anything else she could come up with on the spur of the moment. The girl looked around the room. She had never been in the Boys' Toilets before, and now she knew what she'd been missing. Nothing. The room was completely empty, except for Nick Knuckle, who was restraining her, and Nick's Hench-Persons, Quiff and Germ, who were restraining her friend. Oh, yes! And there was a strange, rather old-fashioned looking boy standing at one of the washbasins, muttering to himself:

"I must have a really good wash, as described in *Biggles Has A Really Good Wash*."

So, apart from six people, it was completely empty.

The girl looked around her, fascinated by the drabness. Her reverie was shattered by the boy.

"Let me go! I've got to . . . you know . . . go! If you don't let me go, I'll go, and then you'll be sorry!"

"Be sorry, will I?" scoffed Quiff, not understanding the boy's pleading. "Oh, dear! I'm really frightened!"

"So am I!" joined in Germ. "I'm so frightened, I could wet myself!" Quiff and Germ hooted with laughter.

"I am doing!" squirmed the boy, uneasily.

Quiff and Germ stopped laughing as the penny dropped. (Or should I say the One New Pee dropped. No, I'll stick to penny!)

"Ugh! Gerroff!" reacted Quiff, thrusting the boy away from him, who promptly rushed into a cubicle and shut the door.

"Don't think you're getting away so easily," said Nick Knuckle, who up until now had not spoken, except to say "Gotcha!"

Realizing that she was surrounded, the girl gulped.

"Doo yoo no hoo I am?" said Nick Knuckle, whose spelling was terrible.

"Er . . . no, sir," replied the girl, who nonetheless had a very good idea.

"Nick Knuckle, the School Bully. Does that frighten you?"

"Yes!" chorused Germ and Quiff, from the heart.

"Not you pair! Her!" yelled Nick, with deep-seated frustration. His choice of Hench-Persons was definitely undermining his credibility as the Toughest Guy on the Block (or in the lavs).

"Right, it's time to initiate them," continued Nick, then realized that the boy was still in the cubicle. "Have you finished?" he yelled at the closed door. The door swung open, bashing Nick on the nose, but fortunately no one noticed, except him of course. It's not easy being a Bully.

"Yes, thank you, sir," replied the emerging First Year, who had, in fact, forgotten to pull the chain. It also seems likely that Nick is not going to give him the opportunity to Now-Wash-His-Hands.

"Right. Get over there with her."

I thought not. So much for Personal Hygiene!

"Right," continued Nick, oblivious to my interruption. "Threaten and scare them, lads!" Germ and Quiff went into a routine of Threatening and Scaring which was both physically exhausting for them and totally unmoving for the First Years. Nick could feel credibility slipping further and further away. He moved on to "Phase Two".

"Right. The Initiation Ceremony. Quiff!" Nick indicated for his trusted Right-Hand Man to take charge.

"Oh. Yeah. Right. Initiation Ceremony. Right. Er . . . well, first you have to take your jackets off."

"No! That's not it! First you roll your trouser-leg up," interjected Germ.

"Do yer? Oh. Yeah. Right. First you roll your trouser-leg up."

"I haven't got any trousers on," the girl pointed

out. The boy wished she had just pretended.

"Oh, no. Yeah. Right. Er . . . " Quiff had never encountered this problem, having limited his bullying to little boys. He found that little girls often hit back.

"Perhaps I could put my coat on back-to-front," the girl suggested helpfully.

"Yeah. That's a good idea," agreed Germ.

"No it isn't!" exploded Nick. "Don't interrupt."

"Yeah! Don't interrupt!" Germ yelled at the girl.

"You, I meant!", Nick yelled at Germ.

"Yeah! Me don't interupt!", Germ yelled at herself. Things were getting confusing.

"Stand on one leg!!!" commanded Nick. Quiff and Germ obeyed immediately, and almost as immediately fell over. Nick was now banging his head on the wall. The First Years were looking concerned. Quiff and Germ were getting up. The Strange Boy was getting washed. I think that's everybody accounted for.

"Right," said Nick, who had calmed down, although his neck had gone completely purple. "Let's show them the Blue Dolphin." Well, you could have cut the atmosphere with a knife. But you would have had to be quick, because almost immediately, the girl said, charmingly: "What's the Blue Dolphin?"

Quiff laughed the mocking laugh of someone who knows something that you don't, especially when that "something" is not very nice, and it's about to happen to you.

"You don't know what the Blue Dolphin is?"

"No, sir."

"HA!", said Quiff, in a way that would have made Vincent Price proud of him. Everyone looked at him. Suspense hung heavy in the air, suspended probably. Everyone looked at each other: Nick at Germ, the boy at the girl, the washer at his soap. Then back to Quiff, who now looked enquiringly at Nick.

"Er . . . what is the Blue Dolphin exactly, Nick?" he said.

It is almost impossible for a human being to explode without totally ruining the decor of the room he or she is in. Nick now achieved the impossible. But, instead of spraying the room with blood and vital donor organs, he sprayed it with words.

"SHOWING THE BLUE DOLPHIN IS WHEN YOU STICK THEIR HEADS DOWN THE LAV!!!" he screeched.

"Oh, yeah! Course it is!" nodded Quiff and Germ.

"How?" shook the girl and the boy.

"How?" enquired Quiff and Germ of their leader.

"Don't you know nothing?" but before they could answer, Nick was demonstrating: "It's easy! Look!"

There wasn't a lot to see, as Nick was now in the cubicle. There was plenty to hear, though. Those who were listening could have taken their pick from the following:

The sound of pleasure, as of someone clearly enjoying shoving someone's head down a lavatory bowl, unaware for the moment that it was in fact their own head.

The gurgling sound of pain and confusion, as of someone having their head shoved down a lavatory bowl, then suddenly realizing they were doing it themselves.

The pulling of a chain, which is slightly more recognizable than the previous two sounds.

Wet hair, which is not an easy sound to listen out for, to be completely honest.

The sound of returning feet, which is what they now all heard. What they now all saw was Nick, decidedly wetter than when he disappeared.

The two First Years realized immediately that the last thing they should now do was laugh. Quiff and Germ did not realize this. In fact, laughing was the very first thing they did. It was also the second, third, fourth and fifth things they did. Nick, who was doing dripping, looking stupid and smelling very badly, now started doing shouting and yelling. This made Quiff and Germ stop doing laughing, and start doing running away, which in turn made Nick start doing chasing after them.

As the lavatory was quite small, it didn't take much running or chasing after before Nick, Quiff and Germ were out of it, leaving the two First Years not laughing, and the Strange Boy washing. And they could have stayed like this, but the Strange Boy finished washing, approached the two First Years, and said:

"D'you know . . . this bar of coal-tar soap has lasted me since June the fourteenth, 1940. Now, that's what I call soap." And with that he left.

"So, that was the Great Nick Knuckle, was it?"

29

said the girl.

"Nah! It was some nutter who likes washing!"

"No. I meant the Bully."

"Oh, him."

"He doesn't seem so tough, does he?" smiled the girl.

"No. You're right. He doesn't," agreed the boy.

"I don't think things are going to be so bad here, do you?"

The boy smiled at her. "No. I think we might be on to a winner, don't you . . . Bonnie?"

"Yes, I think you could be right . . . Clyde."

ELECTION FEVER

It is only the second week of term, and election fever is about to sweep Palace Hill. Normally, of course, Mr Blatherwick the school caretaker sweeps Palace Hill, and he has done for . . . ooh . . . literally *days*. Since the beginning of term, in fact. Five days, if you don't count the weekend; six if you count today. He has actually been school caretaker since 1964. That's a very long time. In fact, for anyone born in 1963, it's almost a lifetime.

Blatherwick was not born a caretaker, but it seemed a natural career move. He was actually an unfrocked Traffic Warden, who pursued traffic offenders with passionate zeal, until he was finally sacked for supergluing cars to the road in no-parking zones, then fining the drivers on the spot (as you know, a spot is all you need!)

On completing his own schooling, Blatherwick had entered the army, where he distinguished himself at marching, and won the Regimental Shouting and Stamping Competition ten years running. He was, however, excused from carrying a gun when a medical inspection revealed that he was a dangerous psychopath. He then carried a large Doberman, called Elliott. The Doberman occasionally carried a gun.

After his military career came to an end, he continued marching (and shouting and stamping) as a hobby, and had high hopes of persuading the Amateur Athletics Association to recognize it as an Olympic event. In fact he wrote to them with this suggestion. He got a very polite reply back, thanking him for his suggestion, but saying that they preferred to limit the marching to the Opening Ceremony. Blatherwick immediately fired off another letter suggesting that, if this was the case, perhaps they could introduce overtaking, so the team who started the Opening Parade wouldn't always be first over the winning line. It was meant to be a competition, after all. Do you know — they never replied. However, having mastered the art of letter writing, he then regularly corresponded with other marchers all over the world, and this had enabled him to gather together the largest privately-owned collection of plantar warts, verrucas, corns and other foot ailments, which he had caringly preserved, stuffed and mounted on plywood, covering the whole lot with sticky-back plastic as demonstrated on "Blue Peter". He regularly exhibited his collection, and blamed the poor attendance at these showings on weak publicity. In his will, he had donated his collection to the

Victoria and Albert Museum, who would probably find somewhere to stick it.

On this particular un-typical Monday (not to be confused with the un-typical Monday mentioned in Chapter One), Blatherwick was not actually in school, but was out road-testing Elliott's new hearing-aid.

The majority of the pupils, however, were in school, though in some cases this was in name only. Of course, there were a few absentees. And tomorrow this would bring in the usual rash of Notes-from-Home — some of them brilliant forgeries, some the genuine article, but all of them along the lines of:

"Dear Mr Grunter, I am sorry Johnnie was not in school yesterday, but he had diarrhoea through the holes in his shoes."

Or: "Dear Ms Wren-Stamper, Spud could not come to school yesterday cus I didn't feel like it. Yours, Mrs Taylor. PS: Mum did write this, honest!"

At the school noticeboard, there was a Smattering of Bullies, eyes pinned to the notice that had been pinned to the Noticeboard that morning. They stared for a while in silence. The silence was finally broken by Nick, who breaks most things.

"What is it?" he asked.

"Paper," replied Quiff, nodding wisely. He had been there when it arrived, and was therefore at an advantage. Of course, he hadn't been just standing there, staring, and waiting for a new notice to arrive. He wasn't *that* stupid. Well, actually, he *was* that stupid. But this particular morning he just happened to be there, syphoning hot water out of the school radiator into his vacuum flask, ready for his mid-morning coffee break.

"It's a notice requesting nominations for a Form Representative," explained Germ, who was not quite as brainless as Quiff. Mind you, you would need some very expensive and accurate equipment to measure the difference.

"What about a Form Executioner?" enthused Nick. "I could be that. I could have a little guillotine in the corner by the nature table."

Germ sighed. "No, Nick. This is an exercise in democracy. Whoever we elect will represent us on the School Council, and argue passionately for us upon such burning issues as not having to wear school uniform."

Nick's face dropped. He picked it up, screwed it back on, made sure the mouth was still working and then spoke: "That could be a problem for me."

"Why's that?" Quiff had suddenly pricked up his ears.

"I haven't got any pyjamas."

Quiff was beginning to wish that he'd left his ears as they were, unpricked. He knew that he was about to embark upon a train of thought which would, like most trains these days, take a very long time to go nowhere. Nick saw the signs written on Quiff's face: the furrowed brow, the crossed eyes, the steam coming from the ears, the forty-foot long placard shooting out of the top of Quiff's head which read: "I'm confused!". Nick realized that he needed to explain.

"I haven't got any pyjamas." he said. "I've only got school uniform. And if I can't wear school uniform I'm going to be cold in bed."

"Not to mention rude at school," Germ pointed out. She was beginning to know about these things.

"Exactly," nodded Nick. "Oh, Germ, if only you could be Form Representative, you could stop them stopping me wearing my school uniform. What a shame I can't put your name down."

"Why not?"

"I can't spell it."

"Oh," said Germ. "Sorry."

"I've got it! We can put Peanut's name down. I can spell that. I've seen it in her vest."

"Have you?" said Quiff, who had been silent for half a page. Quiff's eyes were lighting up (his ears were still pricked). He had totally forgotten for the moment that Peanut was Nick's sister, and thought that looking at a girl's vest label definitely sounded a bit, well, you know, racy. He was being heavily influenced by the tabloid newspapers these days, and was even hoping to study "Scandal" as a GCSE option. Nick could read Quiff like a book, which was amazing, because Nick had never read a book, and therefore had no role model.

"On the washing line," explained Nick, getting back to reading vest labels.

Quiff went pink. "Oh. Right. Yeah." He produced a pencil. "Right. Full name," he said, returning to the matter in hand.

"Peanut, Polyester Warm Wash, Non-Tumble Dry."

Quiff was carefully inserting Peanut's full name in the space on the notice reserved for people's full names, when Madeline bounded up. She was wearing a full hockey kit, and a light sweat.

"Hi, chaps! Missed you on the hockey field this morning!" Germ looked shamefaced. Madeline had that effect on people. She also had the effect of totally exhausting them in about thirty seconds.

"Sorry Mad."

"Apologies are all very well," Mad gushed, "but it's tough playing ninety minutes of hard, furious, no-holes-barred hockey by yourself!"

"Done it!" said Quiff, changing the subject. He'd never liked hockey. He had, however, just put the finishing touches to a very neat lower case "y", which meant that he had now written Peanut's full name. The "y" had been the tricky bit.

"What are you doing?" Mad peered over Quiff's shoulder at the notice.

"Form Representative? Peanut? You are joshing and japing I hope. Here, give me that pencil . . . " She snatched the grubby, blackened stump from Quiff's hand, realized she'd taken his thumb, replaced it, took the pencil instead, and prepared to write. For an educated person like Madeline, preparing to write can take less than a minute.

"I'm going to nominate a born leader," she said, and added the name to the list. "There.

Prince William." Nick looked over her shoulder to check the name. He saw nothing. Wrong shoulder. He looked round for another one. He found it. He checked the name.

"Prince William? What d'you want to nomigranite him for?"

"Because Willy has true grit!"

"Yeah? Well Peanut's got grit too. In her hair!"

And so, the race was on! Although neither of the candidates yet knew it, they were about to be catapulted into an election battle every bit as fierce and dirty as the race to the White House.

Even now, as the Palace Hill election was entering its Primaries Stage, the Presidential Election in America had just come out of the "Don't Vote for him, he's totally mad and wears a wig" stage, and was just entering the "if you vote for me, I'll give you a pencil and a badge" stage. So as you can see, things were Pretty Serious.

The Palace Hill Nomination Form was taken down, taken into the staff room, and taken Very Seriously. Some of the staff felt that, although not all the names on the list were pupils at Palace Hill, they should still have the Democratic Right to be elected, even though some of the nominees had been dead for many years. Among the list of nominees were:

William Windsor (Posh Party)

Peanut Polyester Warm Wash Non-Tumble Dry (Common Party)

Then in alphabetical order:

Michelangelo (Arty Party)

Steptoe and Son (Horse and Carty Party)

Eric Bristow (Darty Party)
The Queen (E R-ty Party)
Baked Beans (Independent)

Then in any old order:

Joan Collins (Party Party)

Ludwig Van Beethoven (Keep Music Live Party)

Band of the Royal Horseguards (Keep Music Loud Party)

Mel Smith (Funny Person Party)

Lord Lucan (Missing Person Party)

Kevin the Gerbil (SDP)

The Full list was finally whittled down to three:

Prince William (Posh)

Peanut (Common)

A Tree (Green)

William's supporters were Madeline, who secretly admired him, Doughnut, who was just a good friend, and . . . erm.

Harry was on Peanut's side, Yob was *by* Peanut's side (she'd taught him to heel beautifully), and Nick was behind her all the way.

PC was a "Don't Know".

Germ was a "Don't Know Nuffink".

Mandy was confused. Her instinct told her that she should stick by William. Her heart told her that she still loved Harry, who loved Peanut. Experience told her that she'd probably forget to vote.

Quiff was also confused. He had little or no idea what was going on.

The teachers, who were allowed to vote, were making a stand and voting for the Tree.

Bonnie and Clyde, who weren't allowed to

vote, were making a fortune selling rosettes, placards, and posters.

But what of the Strange Boy we saw washing in Chapter Four (I know. It seems like years ago, doesn't it?)? Which way will he put his cross? Well, he probably feels that Churchill is doing a splendid job, and that we should leave things as they are. But then, he is not like other boys at the school (or other girls for that matter). Jimmy, for this is the Strange Boy's name, had been a pupil at Palace Hill since the mid-thirties. At the outbreak of war he was evacuated to the West country, along with many boys and girls of his age, but, by skilful use of his I-Spy compass, he was able to find his way back to his beloved school, and had been living in an air-raid shelter in the grounds ever since. Strangely, he did not look a day older than he did in 1940. It's probably the coal-tar soap that does it.

Jimmy had little or no interest in the politics of Palace Hill. He did, however, have a deep abiding interest in the adventures of *Biggles*, and modelled himself on this wartime hero. He also had two goldfish (Monty and Winston), but he didn't want to be like either of them.

But how would the Rest of the School vote?

"Ha! We are in the book after all!"

"Why do you say that?"

"Because, Banana-Brain, he's just said, 'How will the Rest of the School vote?', hasn't he? He wouldn't have said that if we weren't in the book, would he?"

"He might."

"Well, I'm going to change my shirt anyway, just in case. Better to be ready."

"Please yourself. I'm not even going to get dressed."

And on Polling Day, one of the Rest of the School was caught with their trousers down.

THE CAMPAIGNS

Madeline had elected herself to the position of William's Campaign Manager. Mad was a force to be reckoned with. She was the sort of person who would be sitting quite quietly one minute, then, all of a sudden, she'd leap up and yell, "Last one up the Matterhorn is a cissy!" Then off she'd dash, and you wouldn't see her again for a week.

She was bubbling over with ideas: photographs, interviews — she was going to present William as the Ordinary Man of the People, the Neil Kinnock of Palace Hill, only with more hair. There was only one thing left to do. Tell William that she had nominated him.

Peanut had to admit that, by and large, William was more popular than she was. But she couldn't understand it. I mean, he was so low-profile. He never did anything. He never cemented anyone into a wall, tied their legs behind their head, stuck their foot up their nose, nothing. Half the time you'd never even know that there was a Royal Prince at the school. Well, not since the caretaker put up the electrified fence to keep the press photographers away. But nevertheless, unless she did something, William would win without trying. Experience told her that the fairest way to win was to cheat. Well, Nick was already working on that one. But they needed banners, posters, rosettes. They had managed to buy a few from Bonnie and Clyde, but Yob had already eaten those. She confided her problem to Harry.

"Never fear, gentle dove. I managed to raise a few readies for a 'Slush Fund'."

"How?"

"I've sold High Wycombe to the Arabs."

The sleek black Rolls drew to a standstill with barely a sound. The smoked-glass window glided down. Just an inch. Just enough to allow speech and hearing. Not enough to allow the dank, heavy air to enter the thermostatically-controlled interior of the car. The salesman approached the car with the air of someone who knows his place. Someone who is aware of only being a go-between, a middle man. The occupant of the vehicle nodded. This was the indication that communication is permitted.

"Good afternoon, your Imperial Highness. I have here the deed of sale for your signature. Details of all buildings and fixtures are contained in the contract. I must, however, if you will permit me, run through the inventory of accessories:

37 lollipop ladies

4 packs of Venture Scouts

69 milkmen with optional early-morning-wake-the-baby-rattling-milk bottles

73,000 reclining armchairs

45 billion yards of net curtaining

456 million polystyrene ceiling tiles

9,043 miles of neatly clipped privet

14 million freshly washed cars

684,000 babies (assorted sexes)

987,000 OAPs (ditto)

A trouble-maker (there's always one, isn't there?)

Lord Lucan (possibly)

23,800 poodles (definitely)

5,000 pooper-scoopers (fortunately)

17 billion half-finished bottles of medicine . . .

Seven hundred pages later the deal was signed and sealed. That is, once the 524 football supporters and the double glazing salesman had been crossed off the list. Thus, Peanut was off to a flying start.

William was a different matter.

"You seriously expect one to take part in a common election?" had been William's reaction when Mad approached him.

"Well, yes, little Willy! We have to stop Peanut from —"

"Never. Nothing could possibly persuade one to demean oneself with such a public display of . . . Peanut?"

"Yes!"

"That's different . . . hell hath no fury like a

young heir apparent scorned. If it's Peanut I'll run. And I'll beat her!"

"VOTE FOR PEANUT, OR I'LL BITE YER LEG OFF", screamed the poster pinned to the First Years' classroom door, as Doughnut gripped the knob. The poster was an unusually good picture of Yob, with an unusually large number of bad teeth.

"He's eating all the wrong things," thought Doughnut as he turned the knob, pulled, looked embarrassed, put the knob into his pocket and shouldered the door open.

The noise inside the room was loud to say the least. The forty new pupils were currently conducting a scientific experiment to see how many of them could get inside the same desk. They had already spent some time conducting an experiment to discover which cupboard the teacher was cowering in. They had sealed all the cupboards with chewing gum, and then worked out the following equation:

Sealed Cupboards = Shortage of Oxygen
Shortage of Oxygen = Difficulty in Breathing
Difficulty in Breathing = Frantic Banging/ Cries of "Let me out!" from Interior of Cupboard
Frantic Banging etc = Location of Teacher

Simple. They hoped that the Frantic Banging would start before home time, as, if it didn't, it was likely to have stopped again by the morning, and the experiment would fail. Applied science was wonderful.

"Are you electioneering?" asked Bonnie, looking up from the Classified Adverts in the local paper.

"Yes!" Doughnut adjusted his political smile.

"You'll need a soapbox," suggested Clyde, producing a very large one from a very small shoebox on his desk.

"Thank you," stuttered Doughnut.

"And a megaphone," said Clyde, producing one.

"Wow!" exclaimed Doughnut in amazement.

"And some political claptrap." Clyde placed a small article on the desk in front of Doughnut.

"What's that?" enquired Doughnut.

"Clap," instructed Clyde. Bemused, Doughnut clapped. Before he could say "ouch!", the article on the desk leapt up and trapped his hands, like a vice.

"A claptrap," explained Clyde, as if an explanation was needed.

"Absolutely." It was all Doughnut could think of to say. The trap had got his hands, and the cat had got his tongue.

"Just £1.75 the lot," smiled Bonnie.

"Or we won't release your hands," smiled Clyde.

"Money's in the top pocket. Under the beetroot."

"Thanks," said Bonnie, helping herself. "Oh, by the way, Doughnut, do you like food?"

"Well, I have been known to dabble."

"Only we're opening a Tuck Shop."

"Nice." Doughnut stood for a while, then said, "Er . . . do I have to stay like this?"

"Does one have to stay like this, Mad? Only one

feels a trifle foolish, not to say chilly."

It was early morning. It was cold. It was damp. And as far as William was concerned, it was a waste of time. Oh! And it was Madeline's idea: a photocall for William's election campaign.

"But, Willy, yours is the face to secure a thousand votes. Your fisog will look down from a gross of campaign posters pinned to a legion of noticeboards."

"But must it be a photograph?" whined William."One would much rather have one's portrait painted."

"There isn't time," explained the ever-patient Mad. "Besides, this very nice man, Sir Larry O'Lichfield, has agreed to take the snaps."

And indeed, some yards away, there stood what appeared to be a strange nine-legged beast under a black cloth. It swayed back and forth. It was, in fact, Sir Larry O'Lichfield, his two assistants, and his tripod. Take off the black cloth and Sir Larry looked amazingly like Nick Knuckle. His two assistants looked like Quiff and Germ. The tripod didn't really look like anyone in particular.

"Top o' de morning to yers, yer Royal Majestiness, biggorra!" mumbled the nine-legged beast in the worse Irish accent Nick could do. Well, it was the best one Nick could do, but it was still terrible.

"Why are you talking like that, Nick?" said the nine-legged beast to itself.

"Shut up!" it then told itself, and started kicking itself very hard.

"When you've finished your jig, Sir Larry,

could we get on?" asked Mad, rather sharply for her. "Only Prince William has an interview with the School Magazine at ten hundred hours.

"Oh. Roit you are, den, missus," muttered the nine-legged beast. Then turning its lens towards the Prince, it said "Roit, Yer Nerkship, Oi'l just get yers in de frame. Roit. Ah . . . just one step back, please . . . "

"Like this?" queried William, stepping back.

"Oh, very nice, sor. And again, please. And again. Just another. Come on, shift yerself!"

"One is going as fast as one can, Sir Larry O'Lichfield. But, please remember, one only has two feet."

"Yeah? Well get shifting! And another, and another . . . "

Sir Larry's voice grew quieter and quieter, as William's ears got further away from it. William's footsteps also got quieter and quieter as they moved further and further away from the six ears of the nine-legged beast (tripods have no ears). William also got better and better at walking backwards, the more and more he practised.

I think I mentioned earlier that Nick had a plan. If I didn't, I should have done. Anyway, this was it: Getting William to walk backwards. Good, eh? Who knows where it might lead.

Meanwhile, as part of her campaign, Peanut had just been photographed with Nick Kamen, and appeared on the Wogan show. Harry was still having no luck getting her on "Bob Says Opportunity Knocks".

Also, meanwhile, the Tree was refusing to give

interviews, but had been photographed for *Country Life* magazine.

"Another step back . . . and another . . . just another," Sir Larry O'Lichfield's voice was now very faint, but not quite as faint as William felt after so many miles walking backwards.

"One hates walking. It is so pedestrian," muttered William, not really loud enough for anyone to hear. Certainly not loud enough for Nick Knuckle (alias Sir Larry O'Lichfield) to hear, as Nick was some considerable distance away in the playground at Palace Hill.

Not loud enough for Blatherwick to hear either, even though Blatherwick was nearby. Not loud enough for Elliott the Doberman to hear, as Elliott was experiencing a certain amount of teething trouble with his new hearing-aid. The problem, actually, was that Elliott couldn't get his teeth into it to destroy it, as it was guaranteed totally dog-bite-proof.

Road-testing a dog's hearing-aid is not as easy as it sounds.

Blatherwick's first problem was working out exactly how to do it. It was not a topic that had ever been covered by *Blue Peter*, or *Splash* or *Tomorrow's World*. Amazingly, it hadn't even been demonstrated on *Rainbow*.

So, firstly, he had tried tying the dog to a lamp-post, walking a few hundred yards away, and whispering, "Can you hear me?" He then tried *saying*, "Can you hear me?" Then calling, then shouting, then screaming, then leaping up and down yelling, "Can you hear me?" He then eventually realized that the dog could not reply as it did not possess the gift of speech.

A change of plan was called for. Blatherwick decided to call out simple instructions to the dog, such as: "Sit. Stay. Roll over. Beg. Heel. What's wrong with you, you stupid animal, are you deaf or something?" After several hours of this banter, which had the required effect on every dog within a ten-mile radius, but left Elliott totally unmoved, Blatherwick remembered that the only command Elliott was trained to respond to was "Kill!", and this he did brilliantly. So brilliantly, in fact, that he could actually lip-read it. A fact that Blatherwick did not remember until Elliott had attacked three bus drivers, nine lamp-posts and a scout troop, eaten four trollies-full of shopping and a walking-frame.

Blatherwick finally decided that, since he had never had an intelligent conversation with Elliott, the deafness didn't matter. Blatherwick had never had an intelligent conversation with anyone. This was mainly due to the fact that, whatever subject you started off with, Blatherwick could bring the conversation round to 'Marching' in less than five seconds. (His record was 1.76 seconds, when the conversation had started out as Nuclear Physics and its effect on the pound in your pocket.)

Blatherwick returned to the school, throwing Elliott's hearing-aid away as he went. This was later picked up by a tramp, who wore it with pride, and some difficulty — as it was originally designed to be worn by a Doberman. It didn't improve the tramp's hearing, but it did allow him to enjoy, for the first time, such high-pitched sounds as dog whistles, cats being strangled, and Bonnie Langford singing. Lucky tramp!

William's election campaign had ground to a halt, as no one knew where he was. He was in Aberdeen, still going strong — and backwards. But Mad wasn't to know that. She was busy planning the next stage of his campaign — a campaign video. There was only one problem, apart from William not being there, and that was . . .

"The video! It's gone!" exclaimed PC, staring at an empty space that had once been full of video.

LIKE POLLS

"One step back, your Nerdship . . . one more . . . " yelled Nick from the school playground.

"Pardon . . . pardon . . . one can't hear you, Sir Larry O'Lichfield," called William from Foreign Parts.

"One step back," bellowed Nick, rationally. "Look, like this!" he shouted, totally irrationally. Because, although light travels faster than sound, sound travels round buildings, which light doesn't. So, although William could hear Nick (just about), he certainly couldn't see him, on account of the fact that the biggest part of the European Economic Community was getting in the way. Nick didn't understand this. It was just one of the billions of things that he didn't understand. Consequently, Nick continued to demonstrate walking backwards, travelling in exactly the opposite direction to William. And so they both continued for some time.

"The video! It's gone!" repeated PC."

"Oh," said Quiff, at a loss for something intelligent to say, which was nothing new for Quiff.

"We must find it!" PC said, and dashed off with great enthusiasm, but in no particular direction.

"Hmm," said Quiff, still struggling with the "intelligent reply" problem.

Meanwhile, Peanut, using Harry's money, was throwing a Vote Catching and Bribery Party, attended by the Rest of the School . . .

"See! We ARE in the book!"

"Not necessarily."

"We are! He's just said– "

"He's just said there was a party. He hasn't said: 'Meanwhile, at the Party, the Rest of the School were saying such and such, and doing this and that.' Nah. He's just mentioned us in passing. You see. He'll get all the way to the end of the book, and we won't feature once. Nah. Like I say: I'm not even bothering to put my uniform on."

This will prove to be a mistake.

Something else that will prove to be a mistake is Nick walking backwards, although, at the moment, he does not realize this. He is far too preoccupied with concentrating on walking backwards and yelling at William:

"One more step, like this, Your Helplessness . . . one more step . . . just one more . . . " A strange sight. And one that the inhabitants of North America, which Nick has now reached, have never seen before.

Neither have the sheep-shearers of Queensland, Australia, which is where William now finds himself. Not that he is looking for himself. Oh no. He is far too busy concentrating on walking backwards, which he now has down to a fine art. Nick, on the other hand (or rather, at the other end) is struggling a bit. Walking and talking took him until his early teens to master. So, naturally, he finds that walking backwards and yelling at William is a whole new ball-game. Ah! This could be where Nick is going wrong! Walking and talking is not a ball-game at all! Anyway, he's doing his best.

PC did her best in the search for the stolen video, and it paid off. Her search took her, plus a rather confused Quiff, to Jimmy's air-raid shelter, the entrance to which they found entirely by accident. It was Quiff who had the accident. He fell down a hole, which turned out to be the entrance to Jimmy's shelter.

No one (except Jimmy) had ever been into Jimmy's shelter. PC and Quiff were stunned. It was like a wartime Aladdin's Cave. The corrugated iron interior was neatly wallpapered with a large floral-print pattern, partly covered by posters: "Careless Talk Cost Lives!", "Be Like Dad, Keep Mum!", "Put Out That Light!". A large set of flying ducks were flying south, straight into a damp patch, just above the shelves of volumes of *Biggles* books. All the titles were there: *Biggles Beats The Boche*, *Biggles Wins The*

War, Biggles Nobbles The Nasties, Biggles Hits The Hun, Biggles Has A Little Rest — hundreds of them.

"Hello! You're just in time for cocoa!" Jimmy greeted them, holding up his wartime ration of the brown bean. But PC wasn't listening. Her eyes were transfixed by the sight of two small goldfish, apparently swimming around inside her video monitor! Jimmy followed her eyeline.

"Like it?" he enquired, cheerily. "It's my own invention: a musical fishbowl, as described in *Biggles Invents A Musical Fishbowl*," and he pointed to the relevant volume on his homemade shelves (as described in *Biggles Puts Up Some Homemade Shelves*). PC was dumbstruck. But it didn't stop her speaking.

"That . . . that . . . Pico-Pod has turned a twentieth century technological miracle into a musical fishbowl!"

"Good, isn't it? Monty and Winston love it, they're champion jitterbuggers." And so saying, Jimmy pressed the "on" button, causing the strains of Glen Miller's "In The Mood" to issue from the monitor, and the water inside it to swirl lightly, giving the fish a very relaxing whirlpool bath.

"I've always been a bit of a boffin," continued Jimmy, holding up the video recorder, which now had two wire hanging plant-baskets attached to its spools. They were spinning round and round. It was making PC rather dizzy, but that was the shock. Jimmy pointed to the baskets.

"I use this one to dry my lettuce," he continued, "and this one — please excuse the indelicate nature of this disclosure — to dry my smalls."

PC had the sort of hysterical fit that the Americans do so much better than the English. And, after several large mugs of strong cocoa, she had calmed down to a whimpering wreck, but was far from being her usual cheery self.

William was far from being near Palace Hill. He was also far from being near Nick Knuckle, who was himself far from being near Palace Hill.

William was, however, very near a sign which read: "BEWARE! EDGE OF THE WORLD! YES — IT *IS* FLAT!"

Nick, at the other end, was standing very near a similar sign, which read — in a language unreadable by Nick (English) "BEWARE! OTHER EDGE OF THE WORLD! WE TOLD YOU SO!"

At Nick's edge, Nick was yelling: "Just one small step, Your Stupidity!" which went completely unheard at William's edge.

At William's edge, William was calling politely: "Pardon? One can't hear you Sir Larry O'Lichfield!"

"One step back!" Nick yelled at his edge. "Like this!" he demonstrated. "Got it?" he bellowed, from thin air, just one step from his edge of the world. He stood for a second as he took in his situation. He was standing on thin air. His limited knowledge of gravity told him that this was impossible, and so he stopped doing it.

"*Whoosh*!" went the wind in each ear, as Nick fell through space. The wind also untidied his hair rather badly, but he didn't notice. He was far too busy watching his whole life flash before his eyes.

He missed most of the good bits, because he was finding it hard to concentrate. He was preoccupied by the bad bits, of which his present situation was possibly one of the worst. Probably *the* worst. Certainly the *last*, if his limited knowledge of falling from great heights was even partly accurate.

At William's edge, the Heir to the Throne was totally unaware of Sir Larry O'Lichfield's inevitable fate. He was also at a loss as to what to do next. The decision was taken out of his hands by the timely arrival of Mad, who had really got the bit between her teeth. She was also saddled and bridled.

"Hop on, Willy! It's Election Time!" William didn't need to be told twice. He mounted his steed, and rode hot-hoof back to Palace Hill!

PRINCE OF THE PEOPLE

Madeline had promoted William as the "Man of the People", and, really, when he thought about it, he was no different from his school chums. They had holes in their socks. So did he. How else was one supposed to fit one's feet into them? They had no money. Neither did he, although he had had a shot at carrying some. They spoke very very badly. Well, so could he, with a bit of practice. He would ask his father to invite that awfully nice Derek Jameson to tea. One visit should be enough. Oh, yes. William was very confident that he was One of the Boys.

Madeline had had some problems persuading his "chums" that this was the case. Her canvassing had not gone well.

"Can I put you down for Prince William?" She had asked one would-be voter.

"You're joking! He's a bozo! A wally!"

"I see. A Don't Know!" She made a note, then

made her way to the school swimming pool, in an attempt to capture the Floating Voter.

"Excuse me," she said, diving in beside a potential supporter. "Could I ask your voting intentions?"

"Peanut! It's got to be Peanut, definitely!"

"Hmm," thought Mad. "Undecided."

Not too disheartened, Mad lined up one last chance for William to swing the polls — Kissing a Baby.

William was horrified, when Mad broke the news. "Kissing a Baby!!!"

"Yes! It's frightfully good!"

"Yes, it is frightful!"

"But, people like to see politicians kissing babies. It makes them more human!" reasoned Mad.

"What? The babies?"

Ignoring his protestations, Mad wheeled William over to a pram.

"Look, everyone!" she called to any casual bystanders. "Ordinary Prince of the People William is kissing a baby! Isn't that healthy?"

Leaning over the pram, William assumed the role of baby-kisser.

"Coochy, coochy, er . . . coo. Is that right?" The boxing glove that flew out of the pram, on the end of the small but powerful arm, hitting William full in the face, told him that it probably wasn't.

"Where did you get this baby?" complained William.

"It's Yob's kid brother," explained Mad.

"Wha—" William started to say, as Yob's kid

brother pulled him into the pram. William started to kick, not surprisingly. And, also not surprisingly, the pram started to move.

"That pram's going to roll down the hill, you mark my words," said Mandy, who had a rare talent for stating the obvious, which she was now exercising.

"Oh, no! The pram's rolling down the hill!" exclaimed Mad, who had equally good powers of observation. And so it was. William, still stuggling with the baby, was powerless to stop it. On it went, down the hill, missing a dog by inches, and causing the dog to miss a tree by miles.

William may have only missed the dog by inches, but he missed the final count of the School Election completely, as did one of the Rest of the School.

See! You wouldn't listen! I told you we were in the book! But, oh no! You couldn't even be bothered to get dressed! Serves you right!"

"Shut up."

"I have here the results of the Election for Form Representative," proclaimed Mandy in her best Public Speaking Voice.

"A Tree (Green), one vote." This caused a great adult-sounding cheer from the back of the hall, which was immediately "shushed" irritably by the entire school.

"Sorry," mumbled a small adult-sounding group of voices from the back of the hall.

"We won't tell you again!" said the entire school. "Do you want to be kept in?" They then turned their attention back to Mandy, who continued.

"Prince William Hairy Apparent (Posh), no votes."

None? What about Mad? She'd been too busy, organizing his campaign, to vote.

Doughnut, then? He never got out of the clap-trap in time.

And Mandy? She forgot. I said she would.

Back on the platform, Mandy continued:

"Peanut Polyester Warm Wash Non-Tumble Dry (Common) five thousand, four hundred and two votes, out of a possible twenty -seven."

Peanut had had a back-up plan. If the bribery, cheating and threatening had failed . . . forgery. It paid off. Bonnie and Clyde also made enough to open a shop, so it wasn't a total disaster.

William, inside the pram, had reached Basingstoke.

Nick, lost in space, had reached the point where he was telling himself that the falling wouldn't hurt him, as long as he didn't land . . .

THE TRIP

Nick Knuckle was absent from school for ten days. When he did return, the teachers, not surprisingly, did not believe his excuse that he had been abducted by aliens from another galaxy. Mind you, you couldn't blame the teachers. Nick's note-from-home was obviously forged. I mean, he couldn't even remember his mother's surname, even though it was the same as his own.

You couldn't really blame Nick either. Try as hard as he could, he failed to persuade his parents that he really had been abducted by aliens.

"Abducted by aliens! Pull the other one, it's got bells on!" scoffed his mother, when he finally returned home. "Got chatting to some of your pals on the Rec, more like!"

"For ten days?" interjected his father, who realized that chatting to pals on the Rec for ten days was really going too far, even though he actually had little or no understanding of the concept of time. He once bought a sun-dial, and took it back because it had stopped.

"Yes! Ten days! Why not?" continued Nick's mother. "You know what he's like when he gets going!" She then launched into a diatribe about Nick and his shortcomings that lasted four months, seventeen days, five hours and thirty-six minutes, pausing only occasionally for breath, and being sustained by a drip-feed throughout. The media got to hear about it, and in no time at all the house was crammed with film-crews, all living off Nick's Granny's pickle and pilchard sandwiches. Nick's mother was featured on *Record Breakers* with Roy Castle, *Worldwide Record Breakers* with David Frost, but not — amazingly — on *Bob Says Opportunity Knocks*. What is wrong with that man? Needless to say, none of the media folk believed Nick's alien story.

Which was a pity, because it was completely true. Unlike everything I've just told you about his mother, which was completely made up. Sorry.

As Nick fell through space, he wondered how long it would be before he met his inevitable fate. He recalled that Mr Grunter, the Astrophysics and Gardening teacher had explained that space was infinite. That was no doubt true, but it must end some time, and when it did . . . bump!

He wondered what speed he was doing. He recalled his father once explaining a simple method of calculating speed. He remembered the occasion vividly, as it was the only time his father had ever spoken to him.

"You see . . . you look at your watch, and then count the lamp-posts . . . ," explained Nick's father.

"What with?" his son was eager to learn.

"What with what?" said the Expert, wishing he hadn't started this conversation, even if it was the only one he had ever had with his son.

"What d'yer count the lamp-posts with?" continued Nick.

"Oh, I see. I don't know . . . yer fingers I suppose. That's what I use. Seems to work out alright."

"Now how do you look at the watch *and* the lamp-posts?" Nick felt that he may have discovered the one flaw in an otherwise perfect system.

"What yer talking about, yer great —"

"Arthur!" snapped Nick's mother, who was standing nearby, performing minor surgery on next-door's cat. She knew only too well that her husband's vocabulary became very limited when he was cross.

"How do you look at your watch, and count the lamp-posts at the same time?" repeated the pupil.

"Well," said the Expert, struggling to control his temper, "you look at yer watch with yer left eye, and yer lamp-posts with yer . . . er . . . no . . . yer look at yer watch with yer right eye . . . no . . . that's not it . . . which side of the car are you on . . . Right . . . right . . . then yer look at the . . . no . . . the right eye looks at . . . er . . . the road looks at the watch and the . . . no . . . er . . . you put yer right leg in, yer right leg out, in, out, in, out, yer shake it all about . . . "

When Nick's father was well enough to be allowed home, he vowed never to speak to his son again. Not that he ever had before.

On an alien spacecraft, journeying through another galaxy, the aliens were wishing the same thing. They came from the Planet Xfred&bvuypo*lcrfes#, which very roughly translated into English, means Sevenoaks, in the galaxy of Kent, which — again — very roughly translated means Jsrf@edkj.

By the way, if you're trying to speak either of these names, don't bother. The aliens have the three mouths and seven tongues required to speak their language. We don't.

The aliens had been watching Earth for some time, on a satellite dish bought via mail order from the Littlewoods catalogue. They had observed our culture: *Neighbours*, *The Benny Hill Show*, *The Price Is Right*, *Bob's Full House*, etc, and this had taught them that we were a race of inferior beings. They also wrote and complained about *Crossroads* being stopped.

Scooping Nick up as he floated through space had been a bonus for them, not to say a lifesaver for him. They interrogated him for nine days, at the end of which they had not understood a word he had said. They reached the conclusion, wrongly, that they were dealing with a far superior intelligence, and concluded that the TV programmes that they had watched were all part of Earth's defence system (they had heard about "Star Wars"). So they decided to return Nick to Earth before anyone came looking for him. And so, twenty-four hours later, he was safely at home, being ignored as usual by his father.

The pupils of Palace Hill were planning a trip of much 'more modest proportions — a visit to a castle. William and Harry were supervising the loading of the school bus. They were also in the middle of an argument.

"Oh, really, Willy! You can't blame me just because you failed to be selected as Form Representative!"

"Peanut would never have beaten one, if you hadn't been on her side," whinged William.

"Nonsense," replied Harry, knowing that it wasn't. "Anyway. You didn't walk away empty-handed. You were elected Scissor Monitor."

"Yes!" William puffed up proudly. "And one intends to be the best Scissor Monitor Palace Hill has ever known."

"Exactly," toadied Harry. "A Prince among Scissor Monitors."

In a much better frame of mind, William turned his attention towards a group of First Years. "Come on, you lot. It's time to load the boot."

In an alien spacecraft, one of the aliens was adjusting the indoor aerial, as the voice on the screen said:

"Right now it's time for *Bob Says Load The Boot*, the show that puts you in the driving seat!"

The aliens applauded the small screen.

"And can I have tonight's first contestant. Hallo! You are Mavis Dogbite, a pooper-scooper maker from Wednesbury in the West Midlands. Your hobbies include shot-putting and making strange noises with your mouth and other places."

Some of the aliens, the ones that were particular Benny Hill fans, fell off their chairs. One of them then self-destructed with laughter, which sort of spoiled the afternoon's viewing of everyone around him.

Meanwhile, on the small screen: "Your ambition is to travel abroad and shout at foreigners. Is that so?"

"Yes, Bob!" screamed the contestant.

"Correct!"

The aliens who weren't clearing up the mess applauded wildly.

"And, for knowing your name you win the Tupperware Twenty-Inch Television Set and Matching Toilet Roll Holder!"

Sounds of alien envy from the spacecraft.

"And the other contestant: you are Marie Curie, discoverer of Radium, and five times Women's World Darts Champion. Your hobbies include speaking French and juggling, and it says here that you once met Des O'Connor."

More envy from the aliens.

"That's very interesting. What's Des like? Is he as tall as he looks, sitting on that sofa of his?"

"Pardon?"

"No, I'm sorry Marie, that is not the right answer, I'm afraid! But here's what you would have won. Yes! You would have been taking home with you tonight the Principality of Monaco! Never mind! Right! Now you all know the rules. You must load the boot as fast as possible, eating any luggage left over at the end, then complete the following sentence, in less than ten words: 'I like making a wally of myself on television because . . . ' Any questions?"

"Where do babies come from?"

"Right! The time starts now!"

One of the aliens untwizzled the thing that passed for his arm, and changed channels. They heard: Xfvdhgu$rc kuhjgx# fds kugv*mjhght ctr nht&rfg!!! bfsljoya*vjfuyjvhor?? cyjtf! That's right! They were watching the Colbys!

The pupils of Palace Hill were far too excited about the school trip to watch the Colbys. In the corridor Nick and Quiff were making their way towards the coach. They suddenly became aware of being followed by a vision in pink gingham.

"Who is it?" whispered Nick, not very quietly.

"It's me, Germ," said the Pink Vision.

"Nah! You can't be! Germ's a bloke!" replied Quiff.

"No he's not! He's a girl. I know, because I'm him."

"Cor!" Quiff was always one for the intelligent response.

"You'd better not let people see yer dressed like that. They'll talk," advised Nick.

"Of course they won't! I'm a girl. I'm supposed to dress like this. For too long I have denied my femininny . . . er . . . feminitty-tinny . . .

femininniminnitinny . . . er . . . girlness.
Well, not any more. From now on I am going to
dress in a manner that befits a girl on the
threshold of blossoming womanhood."

"Well, I think you look very nice," said Quiff.

"D'you want a smack in the gob?" replied the
Pink Vision.

Elsewhere, everyone was making their way to
the coach. Jimmy was fully prepared for any
eventuality. He had packed a small rucksack with
plasters, cocoa, useful string, a box of matches,
I-Spy compass, powdered milk, powdered egg,
powdered bacon, powdered potato, sleeping bag,
extra blankets, and, of course, a large flask of tea.

"Got to make sure I'm not caught short, as
described in *Biggles Makes Sure That He's Not
Caught Short*," explained Jimmy to anyone
who'd listen.

PC was armed with her (recovered) video
equipment. She was determined to capture this
bit of English history on tape.

Bonnie and Clyde were armed with a street
trader's barrow. They were determined to make
another killing.

At the coach, everyone filed on, having firstly
been stopped by William.

"Scissor check," explained Princess Diana's
Number One Son.

You checked mine earlier, Guvner. I'd lost
them," said Doughnut, helpfully. He then
climbed aboard.

"Mandy?"

"You're taking this Scissor Monitor business
very seriously, William," she said, holding out her

scissors.

"Of course! One day I will be King."

"Oh." She'd never thought about it like that. But then, I suppose she wouldn't as she has no chance of ever being in line for the throne of England, or anywhere else for that matter.

"Tick me, Willy!" called Mad, as she bounced past, scissors aloft.

If only everyone was as efficient as her, William had cause to reflect as the rest filed past, with their various excuses.

"Scissors? No. But I've got my ration book," said Jimmy.

"Scissors? Sure! What kind would you like? asked Clyde, opening his coat to reveal rows of scissors inside. William was just recovering from this when PC arrived.

"Listen," she began, "I've made a bomb. I was bootstrapping at kilobaud, and I got so much babble, that my scissors snipped my bistable, OK?"

"If you say so," replied William, rather lamely. Ah well, at least everyone was now on board. Everyone, that was, except Harry and Peanut (and Yob of course). To make matters worse, they were sharing one of those little intimate moments that can be very annoying to anyone on the outside. Especially if that person on the outside wants to be on the inside, as William did. To see them standing there, wrapped up in their own little world, made him so angry that he almost started to feel . . . to feel . . . an emotion. Gosh. He would have to "play it cool". That was probably the expression. Yes. He'd do that, whatever it meant. He wouldn't let them see that they were getting to him. He'd pretend that he thought the whole thing was really rather childish and immature. He'd rise above it. Yes. That was it. Rise above it. Yes. After all, he could always have a little cry in private later.

"Come on, you two," he said, putting on his best "who cares" sort of voice. "It's time to stop canoodling."

"We weren't canoodling, clever Dick," said Peanut, in a manner guaranteed to hurt (or your money back). "We were discussing our scissors, actually."

"Yes!" snorted Harry, unpleasantly. "We were making cutting remarks!" Then they breezed past him on to the coach. William would not reply. He would not stoop to their level. He bit his lip.

Yob bit his leg.

William limped on to the coach to discover that all the seats were taken, except the one directly over the wheel-arch. You know the one — the one that makes you feel sick. He sighed a philosophical sigh.

"Are we all here?" he began.

"Quiff's not all here!" hooted Harry, to which Peanut laughed far harder than the joke warranted. Why do people do that when they're in love, thought William. Nevertheless, he wished she was doing it to his jokes.

"Oh, by the way," called out Nick slightly embarrassed. "The bloke in a skirt is Germ, OK?"

"What's that smell?" Quiff asked Germ, who was sitting next to him.

"It's de-odorant," she replied.

"What's de-odorant?" her travelling companion then wanted to know.

"I've got it in my armpits," she told him.

Quiff thought for a second. "That's funny. I've got hair in mine." He sat back, considering this new information. He believed that he had now discovered the difference between the sexes. He would pass this on to Nick at some convenient moment.

"Where are we going, Guvnor?" Doughnut enquired of William, who was still standing up looking important.

"We're going to a castle that once belonged to Rob Roy."

"Yes," quipped Harry. "We're going to rob Roy Castle!" Again the over-enthusiastic response from Peanut.

"Wouldn't have thought he had anything worth nicking," commented Nick, to no one in particular.

"We're ready to leave, sir, miss," said William politely to the two teachers huddled on the back seat of the coach. There was no response. William coughed discreetly. They seemed to be preoccupied. William could now feel all eyes staring at him enquiringly. William pointed vaguely in the direction of the teachers and explained.

"They're . . . er . . . marking books." This met with knowing nods all round, particularly from Quiff, whose book got marked more than most. In fact, sometimes the teacher wrote more in it than he did.

As the coach pulled away, Mandy stared out of

the window. She was miles away:

The sky was the same blue as a peacock's feather. The sun a bright ball of 22 carat gold. The sea was so clear that you could see to the bottom, where the sand was like grains of precious metal, hewn from the earth. A light breeze caused the palms to waft almost imperceptibly. What cloud there was hung in the hazy sky like little drifts of pure white snow. As she moved dreamily along the beach, feeling the fine, soft sand between her toes, and the hot sun playing on her skin, she knew she had found a perfect haven. Then, in the distance, she noticed a familiar sight, hanging like a mirage in the heat-haze. Were her eyes deceiving her? Could it be? It was. As she drew nearer, she knew. The firm young limbs, the tousled mop of reddish hair, the boyish freckles, the strong jutting Adam's apple. It was him. Should she speak? Or should she wait until he noticed her? No. She would speak. Why not? Well, here goes, she thought to herself as she drew breath, her heart pounding in the heat:

"Hello! It's Roger, isn't it? Roger Simkins, whose mother is a martyr to her ingrowing-toenail? I thought so, cus you used to live up by the Coin-Op Launderette, didn't you? I'm doing my School Project on ingrowing-toenails, actually. Perhaps your mother could browse through it and give me a few pointers. What a lovely tan you've got.

Almost the same shade as a shoe-dye I used once. 'Rampant Ox' it was called, and it was supposed to give your shoes that 'Living Leather Look', but, do you know, it took three and a half weeks to dry, and even then left a brown ring on my socks. A friend of mine swears by 'Pad-A-Dye', but I don't know, I think it's all swings and roundabouts. What do you think, Rodge? Do you mind if I call you Rodge, Rodge?"

But "Rodge" had buried himself alive in the golden sand, beneath the tropical sun.

Outside the castle, the coach juddered to a standstill, as the driver inadvertently threw the gears into reverse while looking for first, not for the first time. The worst time it had happened was when they had been coming along the motorway at 134 miles an hour. The driver had wanted to change gear, had thrown the gear into reverse, which in turn had thrown most of the inhabitants of the coach into each other's laps, and most of the hand-luggage on to William's head. This had resulted in annoyance from William and an immediate scissor check.

A third scissor check was in progress as Mandy came out of her reverie and joined the others coming out of the coach.

"Let's play hide and seek," enthused Mad. "Last one to hide is a bad egg!" And off she rushed.

"If they're a bad egg, they'll be easy to find!" snorted Harry, much to the delight of his Greatest Fan.

"I've still lost my scissors, if you're interested Guv," said Doughnut, noticing the far away look in William's eyes.

"Oh. Yes. Thanks."

"I say," this was Jimmy, and he did say. "I say, let's go exploring, as described in *Biggles Goes Exploring*." And he did go exploring.

The First Years, Bonnie and Clyde, unloaded their barrow, and headed off to look for some tourists.

Since the teachers were still "marking books", William decided that he had better take charge.

"I think we should all stick together," he said rather limply.

"What a dump," said Nick, in the direction of the castle.

"Wow! Mega-mega-flop! We don't have anything like this in the States!" exclaimed PC, as she aimed her video at the castle.

"You're lucky." Nick again.

"Right. Listen up, chums. In the . . . er . . . absence of the teachers, I, as Scissor Monitor, am taking charge."

"Peanut's the Form Rep," pointed out one dissenter.

"Yeah," agreed another.

"I think you'll find she's busy," said William, with more than a hint of venom.

"Oh. Fair enough," was the general reaction.

"Right. Form a line behind me. That way we won't get lost." They sort of did this.

"As one is the only one with a guidebook, one will show us around, pointing out any interesting facts as we go. OK, yah?"

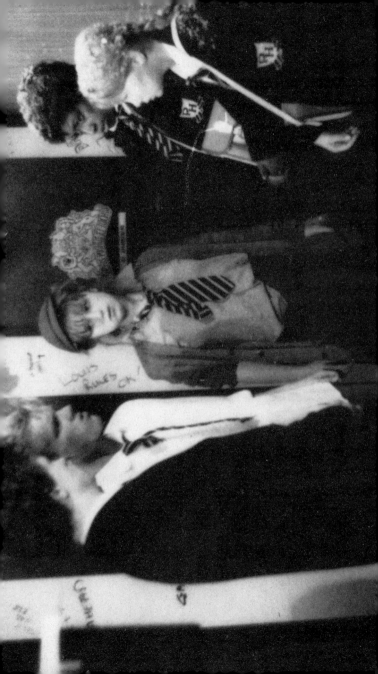

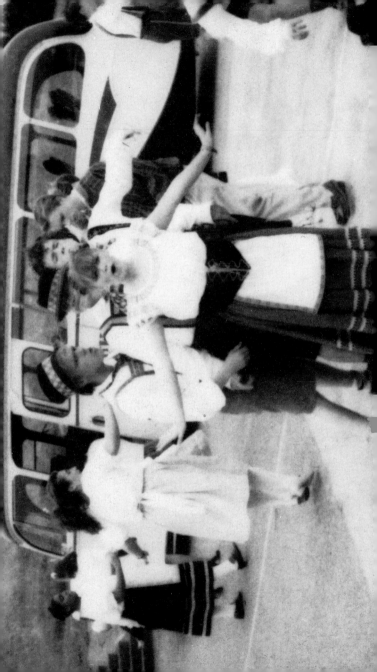

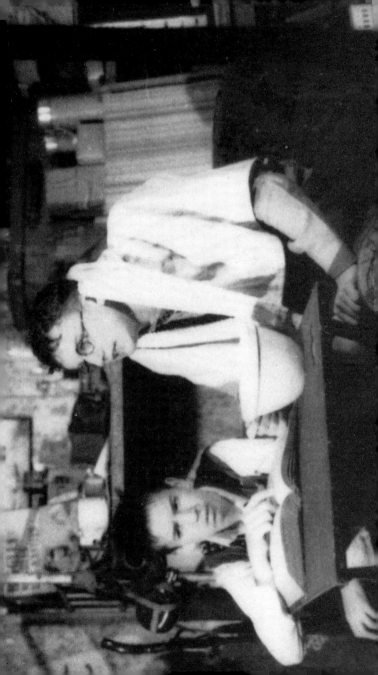

"If you like," seemed to be the consensus of opinion.

"Right. Here goes." And William launched into the history of the castle, as the crocodile moved slowly along the winding path leading up to the castle keep. The path was flanked with bushes, walls and trees. Just the sort of places that people could dive into, over or behind, if they either wanted to be alone, or just simply wanted to get away from someone else who was boring them stupid. Consequently, when William reached the castle keep, he found that he was entirely alone.

One of the useful bits of information that everybody missed William telling them was that the castle, called Castle Hardley, was built by the Dukes of Hardley shortly after the Norman invasion, in 1066. It fell down a week later, since none of the Dukes knew anything at all about building. The castle that stands on the site now dates from the fifteenth century. (It took them that long to find a decent builder, who was cheap.)

They also missed this interesting anecdote: Between the north wall of the keep, circa 1400, and the fire hydrant, circa 1957, is the very spot where the fourteenth Earl of Hardley, Sir Winnalot Du Prey, met his untimely and grizzly end. He was mercilessly and brutally cut down in his prime, with a bunch of disappearing flowers, by an irate Children's Entertainer at his son's fourth birthday party. And all he did was call out, "It's up your sleeve!"

"Isn't that interesting?" commented William to

his "chums". But they were no longer there. They had completely disappeared into thin air — a much better trick than anything seen at Sir Winnalot's son's fourth birthday party.

So. He was alone. Alone and lonely. And lost. A lost soul. A loser in love, a loser in politics. And now a loser in the Fickle Friendship Game. Being Special brought with it its fair share of heartache, he was about to think . . .

FLASH! FLASH! FLASH!

"Over here, William!"

"This way, please, your Highness!"

"Just a bit more ankle, now!"

Oh, no! The Press! Suddenly the self-pitying was forgotten, as William followed an in-built Royal instinct that was passed on in the blood. An instinct that high-bred people shared with the humble fox, hare and deer that they were so fond of chasing. He ran like hell.

"Come back, please sir! I'm Warmth of the *Sun*!"

"I'm Syne of *The Times*!"

"I'm Plunkett of the *Beano*!"

Jimmy was in the middle of his exploring. "Gosh! Look! Crikey! I've found a knight's helmet with a funny pointy bit, as described in *Biggles Finds A Knight's Helmet With A Funny Pointy Bit*. He put it on, and immediately wished he hadn't since he couldn't get it off again. In true wartime spirit, he decided to make the best of the situation, and set off to explore. The first thing he explored was a wall. He studied it very closely. He walked straight into it.

Doughnut was in his element. Being a "townie", the trip to the country had been full of new experiences for him. The things he had seen! A tree! Flowers! A lake! Horse manure! The sort of things you only read about in books. Or so he'd heard, never actually having read a book himself. Although, of course, knowing my luck, he'll probably read this one, just to make sure that I haven't libelled him.

He had also found a larder, with a seemingly endless supply of food. That was the highlight of the day so far. However, he expected that the highlight of the day would, finally, turn out to be the *eating* of the seemingly endless supply of food.

Not being a selfish person, he was currently sharing some of this food with a handful of ducks, another new experience (although he had had duck from the Chinese takeaway, but it wasn't quite the same thing).

It was here beside the lake feeding the ducks that Mandy found him. She had not been looking for him. She had actually been looking for a quiet spot to read her magazine.

"Hello, Doughnut," said Mandy to Doughnut.

"Hello, Mandy," said Doughnut to Mandy. "What have you got there?" he asked, pointing to her magazine.

"It's my magazine 'Teenage Trauma'. It has become my Highway Code to guide me down the avenue of life. I also use it to line my hamster cage. Look, here's a typical article: 'Teen-Quest: Get To Know The Real You That Lurks Beneath The You You Show The World'."

"What is it?" asked Doughnut, fighting off the ducks, who were feeling left out of things.

"It's a questionnaire. Let's do it together."

And they did it together.

While Doughnut and Mandy were filling in the questionnaire, William was being pursued by the Press, and Jimmy was bumping into things, Nick, Quiff and Germ were wandering around the castle interior. They were currently in a room labelled "Tudor Bedroom", which was all nicely laid out in the way that history tells us a Tudor Bedroom would be all nicely laid out. Except, of course, there were thick red ropes around everything, preventing ordinary people from getting anywhere near.

Quiff, who was learning a little about History, was impressed. Nick wasn't. Germ was trying to have a conversation with a dummy dressed as Anne of Cleves.

"I said, do you know where the Ladies is? You deaf or something?"

"Boring, this is," said Nick, having given the room the benefit of his worldly experience (after all, he had been to another galaxy). "I mean," he continued, "They ain't even got no shelves. Where are they going to put their video? Tell me that."

"They don't have videos," explained Quiff, talking about the Tudors as though they were still around, which, of course, they may well have been, as far as Quiff knew.

"Cor! No videos? They have it tough, those Tudors, don't they?"

"The Ladies, I'm looking for." Germ was very persistent.

"And that rope round the bed. That's a mistake. Suppose you wanted to go to the lav in the middle of the night. You could break your neck on that, couldn't you?"

"Nah! They don't have to go to the lav in the middle of the night. They have someone to do that for them."

"Someone to go to the lav for them? Cor! That's clever!" It seemed the perfect system. But there had to be a flaw. Nick thought he knew what it was:

"How do they know which one to do?"

Quiff was caught off guard. "Eh?" he said.

"Cus, if they did the wrong one, you'd still want to go, wouldn't yer?"

Quiff had never thought of it like that. "I'd never thought of it like that," he confessed.

"Yeah, you see. It's not all it's cracked up to be, Royalty, is it? I mean, I've seen castles with no roofs. Some of them haven't even got all their walls. You see, they get ripped off by builders just like the rest of us."

"Yeah. Cor," offered Quiff.

"You're asking for a smack in the cake-hole," Germ warned the Dummy, and stalked off.

Nick and Quiff made a mental note to be nicer to William and Harry, wherever they were. Their brains being what they were, of course, the mental note had gone by the time either of them came to read it.

William was still being pursued by the Press, but

had given them the slip by darting into a priest's hole. In the darkness he relaxed, secure in the knowledge that he would never be found.

"Thank heavens," he murmured quietly to himself, believing himself to be alone.

"Oh, clever old you, Willy! You found me!" cried a strangely familiar voice from the dark.

"What?" said the startled William.

"I suppose I'll have to pay a forfeit! What's it to be? Fifty press-ups? A hundred? Two thousand?"

"No! Nothing! I didn't even know you were . . . " William rushed from the dark little place without even finishing his sentence, let alone setting Madeline a forfeit. He tumbled out into the bright sunshine to be met by . . . oh no! Harry and Peanut, who were bound to misinterpret his actions.

"Hello, hello, hello!" grinned Harry, practising for a career in the Metropolitan Police. Peanut giggled and pointed. I don't know what she was practising for. William just blushed and ran off, hotly pursued by Mad.

"Don't be silly, Willy!" she called after him, and they were gone.

"Well, well, well," smirked Harry.

"Mono sodium glutamate," said Yob, eating a book, and reading a crisp packet.

"Isn't he supposed to eat crisps and read books?" suggested Harry.

"Yeah, but he's confused, ain't he?" explained Peanut.

"Thiamin," continued Yob. Harry had to think of a way to get rid of him. He was sick of Yob playing gooseberry.

"Peanut?" he began, gingerly.

"Yeah?"

"I wish . . . I wish we were alone."

"We are," replied the Love in his Life.

"Polly-un-saturates," said the Thorn in his Side."

"No. I mean that one would like to be . . . completely alone."

"Completely alone?" Peanut struggled to follow his thread.

"Ribo-flavin," Yob struggled with his crisp packet.

"Yes."

"You mean, with nobody else here?" I think she had caught on.

"Exactly!" Harry thought so too.

"Fair enough," she said, and left. She hadn't.

"No! Just a minute!" Harry protested to the disappearing figures of Peanut and Yob. "I didn't mean . . . oh, why is this love business so sticky?"

Mandy and Doughnut had completed the questionnaire, after a few false starts.

"Right!" said Mandy, "let's see how we've done."

"Right," agreed Doughnut.

"Check your scores," read Mandy. "Nought to five points: you are absolutely sure of your femininny . . . femininnitinny . . . femininnitinnininny . . . er . . . girlness." She turned to Doughnut, blushing lightly. "Or, in your case, boyness." she giggled.

"Five to ten points: you could try harder to be

more assertive," she continued to read. "Ten to fifteen points: oh, dear, you really are a bit of a mess aren't you?" she turned to Doughnut.

"Right, what did you score, Doughnut?"

"One thousand, seven hundred and forty-two," he mumbled. Mandy thought of something to say.

"Oh, dear." Well, it was something, if not much.

Doughnut could read her thoughts. "Yeah. I'm just a mess," he said, shredding the remains of the duck-bread in his hands.

"No you're not!" Mandy protested, a little too shrilly. "Not at all. You're really *not*!" she over-emphasized. Doughnut was encouraged by this.

"Aren't I?" he said, beginning to perk up.

"No, not at all," Mandy reiterated. "You're just very, very, very, very, very, very, very, very, very, very, very, very, very, very, very, very, very, very fat!"

"Oh."

"Yes! But you could diet! And then all your problems would melt away like unwanted unsightly fat!"

"Yes! Of course! You're right! I will! I'll diet!"

"Great!"

"Tomorrow!" said a far more positive Doughnut, as he jammed an entire Dundee cake, sideways, into his mouth.

Germ had had a terrible day. Perhaps femininny . . . femininnitinny . . . feminitti-tininittinny . . . girlness wasn't such a good idea, after all. Everywhere she went, people told her how pretty she looked. She'd never been in so many fights in one day before. She decided to hide away in the Ladies. At least she would be safe in there.

As she entered, she heard the sound of someone singing the most beautiful love song ever. At least, she supposed that it was beautiful. Beautiful love songs were not her strong point. They usually made her go "Yuck!" This one made her go "Yuck!" as well. So logic told her that it must be a beautiful love song. Thank you logic, she thought. Yuck! It was enough to make you sick. She couldn't understand why everyone was into this love rubbish. Mandy loved Harry. Harry loved Peanut. William loved Peanut. Mad loved William. Doughnut loved Food. Bonnie and Clyde loved Money. Nick loved bashing people. PC loved Computers. Quiff loved History. Yob loved books. You couldn't get away from it.

She suddenly realized that, despite herself, she was tapping her toe and mouthing along to the words of the love song. Perhaps this love was catching. She hoped not. It made people go very stupid. She shook herself out of her daydream, just in time to miss Bonnie leaving the lavs. If she had seen Bonnie, she would have wanted to know why Bonnie was staring at her, and why Bonnie had suddenly dashed off in a tearing hurry.

She didn't, however, miss Mad coming out of one of the cubicles, still singing. So it was *her* doing the yucky singing.

"I didn't know you could sing," she commented to Mad, who was Now-Washing-Her-Hands.

"Oh, yes. I learned it in the Guides," replied

Mad, looking around for the non-existent hand-towel, then drying her hands on her running shorts. "I got my Advanced Singing Badge."

"Oh," said Germ, with no enthusiasm. She thought singing was a waste of time. Mainly because she couldn't do it herself.

"I must say," gushed Mad, "that you're looking jolly pretty."

"You musn't," warned Germ. "Cus the next person who says that will get shown my breakfast."

"Gosh!" replied Mad, forcing a polite smile, but feeling slightly sick.

"Roll up! Get your Castle Hardley memorabilia here! Tee-shirts! Mugs! Key rings! Toilet bags! Place mats! Drink coasters! Pencils! Nodding dogs!" Clyde was doing a roaring trade with his barrow in the picnic area, when Bonnie came rushing up.

"Clyde, Clyde! I've just heard Germ singing!" she called out breathlessly.

"Oh, no! Poor you! D'you want to buy some ear-plugs?"

"No! You don't understand! She was brilliant! And it gave me a great idea! I was thinking that, with her voice, and her new image, she could be the Pop Sensation of the Eighties! Bigger than Kylie Minogue! Younger than Tiffany!"

"Louder than Bonnie Langford?" suggested Clyde."

"Well, no! But you can't have everything!" Bonnie became more businesslike. "Now, what we must do is get her under contract."

That proved to be the easy part. Germ had no idea what they were talking about.

"Look," advised Bonnie, when they finally tracked her down. "Don't worry about the small print. Just sign at the bottom, and the world will be your oyster."

"D'you think the world could be my super-duper whoppa-mega-burger with dill pickles in a sesame seed bun? Only I don't like oysters," requested Germ.

"Of course!" lied Bonnie. "Just sign the contract!"

"A cross will do," suggested Clyde, helpfully.

And so Germ signed. And she discovered what it was that she loved . . . FAME!

It was a much more positive group of pupils who returned to the coach that evening. Several decisions had been made that would change the course of their lives. Germ was going to become a major pop star, with the help of Bonnie and Clyde. Bonnie and Clyde were going to become very wealthy, with the aid of Germ. Germ, although she didn't yet know it, was going to need the help of Madeline. Madeline was going to make more of an effort to get herself noticed by William. William was going to make more of an effort to overcome his love for Peanut. Peanut was going to make more of an effort to stop Yob eating everything. Which brings us to Doughnut. Doughnut was going to make a real effort to diet, helped by Mandy. Mandy was going to throw herself into helping Doughnut, in order to take her mind off Harry. Harry was going to sort out his relationship with Peanut. Peanut's brother Nick was going to, er . . . he'd forgotten. And Quiff was going to help him do it.

PC would probably video it all.

But what about Jimmy? Well, he was still stuck inside the knight's helmet with the funny pointy bit, and would remain so, until he was able to obtain a liberal application of petroleum jelly, as described in *Biggles Obtains A Liberal Application Of Petroleum Jelly*.

The teachers were going to need a rest. The coach was going to need a push, and the Press were going to need a story. That wouldn't be so difficult. It was just a question of finding a local person, buying him a drink, and letting him talk.

Next day, several newspapers carried the banner headline: "The Royal Princes I Have Never Met". There then followed an "exclusive" interview with a gardener from Hardley Castle, who had had the day off and missed the Royal Visit completely. The story stretched over ten pages, with photographs of his wife, his cat, his stuffed gerbil, and his very fine collection of pre-war-toe-clippings. Newspaper circulation trebled.

Which only goes to prove that nothing is impossible. An encouraging thought for the pupils of Palace Hill.

GOING FOR IT

It is amazing how fast the euphoria of
enthusiasm can disappear. I expect some great
brainey person has worked out an equation to
demonstrate this. Why, even now, Erno Rubik is
probably turning it into a puzzle. If he can be
bothered.

Amazingly, only Doughnut stuck to his guns,
and his diet. Oh, and it would be fair to say that
Mandy helped.

As for the others, well . . .

Another totally untypical Monday morning
found them all in class, studying the homemade
covers on their exercise books. Harry stared at
his, and shook his head:

"Gosh! Look at the state of this ermine. It's
almost an endangered species."

"So is this brush nylon," agreed Peanut.

"And this terry towelling," countered Mad.

"So's this pink gingham." Guess who!

"So's this lettuce." Doughnut was taking his diet very seriously.

"What's your book covered with, Yob?" asked Mandy.

"Teeth-marks," he said, and ate it.

"It's terrible," said Harry.

"Needs more salt," said Yob.

"Something must be done about the state of the school equipment, eh, William?"

All eyes turned to the far corner of the room, where William had now taken up almost permanent residence.

"Everyone got their scissors?" he muttered, weakly. Everyone looked despairingly at each other. William had been like this now for over a week. He was keeping himself totally apart from the others.

However, something did have to be done about the lack of school equipment. Peanut decided to assert herself as Form Representative.

"Right, listen everybody," she said, standing on a chair.

"Who's turn is it with the pencil?" asked Mandy, who was trying to construct a weigh-loss chart for Doughnut.

"Listen, everybody," Peanut repeated, impatiently. Harry leapt to her aid.

"Pray silence for the Form Representative!" he yelled.

"Button your lip," she said sternly. She had not forgiven him for sending her away at the castle, or given him the opportunity to explain. Had William observed this, he would have realized that their relationship was definitely on the skids.

Unfortunately, William was far too busy staring into space to notice anything. Yes. Something *was* going on in his head, but nothing short of major brain surgery would discover what it was. Harry, however, could be read like a book.

"I think we've just had our first tiff," he murmured to no one in particular. He was right. And it would not be the last.

"Listen," continued Peanut, ignoring Harry's mutterings. "We need to lay our hands on some new school books."

"Yes, indeed! chirped Harry. "I vote that we go out and buy some!"

"Buy some!" Peanut was amazed. "I see, theft not good enough for you, then, Posh Pants?" Harry decided that it would be better to keep his mouth shut. He was right again. Mandy realized this.

"Harry's right!" piped up Mandy. She would do anything to get into his good books, even if they were a bit tatty. "What we need is a good fund-raising scheme!"

Everyone agreed, very enthusiastically, especially Mad: "Super-duper wheeze! Bags I be the Money-Counting Monitor! Last one to a million is a cissy!"

Faced with such overwhelming support for the scheme, Peanut couldn't really do anything else other than agree, even though she knew she'd never live it down at the Hell's Angels.

It is truly incredible how people will throw themselves into something, when the end result is something that they deeply believe in. Namely *money*.

William, despite all his attempts to keep himself to himself, got caught up in the proceedings. He started walking to school, just to see what it felt like. On this particular morning, he rather wished that he hadn't.

Above the school gate hung a large sign, reading (for those who could) "ELEPHANT EARS DAY". PC and Quiff were manning a small homemade turnstile at the gates.

"What's all this?" asked William, when they stopped him.

"Well," explained PC, "let me download you the format: you're allowed to come to school today wearing Elephant Ears, but you have to pay 50p to the School Fund. So, let's get elastic with the bread."

William looked totally confused.

"She means you owe us 50p," explained Quiff, who was beginning to speak the language.

"But these are one's own ears!" protested the Prince. "One has had them all one's life!"

PC's eyes lit up. "You mean you wear them every day?"

"Certainly," said William, not realizing the way her mind was going.

"Wow! Mega-bucks!" she chuckled gleefully, producing a calculator. "Let's see, 50p a day, 365 days a year, how old are you, to the nearest pound?"

"Oh, no! Look, one is awfully sorry, but one doesn't carry money. However, one may be able to arrange to get you Elgin's Marbles."

"We'd rather have his dart-board!" quipped

Quiff.

This was just one of the bright ideas that people had to raise money. Some of the others were even worse.

Yob organized a Sponsored Reading, and Eating, of the Complete Works of William Shakespeare.

The Knuckle Gang visited the local Playgroup, to try their hand at extortion. But Nick got threatened by one of the children there, and they came away empty-handed.

And, of course, Doughnut was on a Sponsored Diet. Mandy organized an Official Public Weigh-In. Jimmy had devised a homemade "I Speak Your Weight" machine, as described in *Biggles Devises A Homemade I Speak Your Weight Machine*. It consisted of a plank, with a First Year lying underneath it.

Doughnut stepped onto the plank.

"Ouch! Gerroff, you fat slob! You weigh a ton!" said the "I Speak Your Weight" machine.

"A ton?" queried Doughnut, alarmed. "But I only weighed 25 stones before I started!"

"You've obviously got further to go than you thought," sympathized Mandy, jotting his weight down on her chart. She was obviously going to need a bigger chart.

Meanwhile, Germ was wondering whether fame had passed her by. It certainly seemed a long time coming. Maybe it had come and gone, and she had missed it. After all, she had no idea what it looked like. She had heard that it could be a Cruel Master, whatever that meant. She challenged

Bonnie and Clyde about it, the next time she saw them.

"Of course we're going to make you a star, Germ," assured Bonnie, when Germ interrupted her as she was supervising the building work in their tuck shop. "Just as soon as you bring us a demo tape."

"Demo tape!" gulped Germ.

"Yeah," said Clyde. "After all, we must have something to play to Stock, Aitken and Watercress,"

"Waterman," corrected Bonnie, glaring at him.

"Yeah. Exactly. Good old Dennis!" smiled Clyde.

"Oh. Right," said Germ.

"Yes. You bring us a tape of your singing, and we'll do the rest. Now, if you'll excuse us." And with that they left Germ standing, and wrestling with her one big problem. Which was: how could she give them a tape of her singing? She couldn't sing! She had worked out some time ago that Bonnie must have heard Madeline singing, thought it was Germ, and offered her the contract. So, if she wanted to be famous, she certainly had a problem.

Unless she could get a tape of Madeline singing . . .

Anyone taking part in the Sponsored Run Round The Hockey Field, organized by Madeline, would have been very surprised to see Germ burying a microphone into the ground, then laying the lead along the ground and round behind a bush. They would have been surprised

(A) because it was a strange thing to be doing, and (B) because she was doing it nowhere near the hockey field, for the very reason that there was a sponsored run going on. She was not *that* stupid. Not quite.

No. She was burying the microphone, with the talking-into bit (she didn't know the proper technical term) sticking up out of the ground, just at the very spot where she knew that Mad was going to perform her Sponsored Press-ups. She had also bribed a particularly hard-up Second Year to suggest to Mad that she might like to sing as she exercised. Germ just had to hope that this same Second Year didn't decide to sell their story to the Sunday papers, when Germ was Famous. How many other skeletons did she have in her cupboard, that might come tumbling out, the minute she tasted stardom? What about the goldfish that died because she forgot to feed it? And the time she put the newspaper through the wrong letterbox by accident? And the 10p she found lying in the road that she . . . the list was endless! She shuddered. Maybe it wasn't such a good idea to be famous after all. Yes, it was. It was what she wanted more than anything.

She was shaken out of her private thoughts by the approach of Mad. Germ dived behind the bush and started the tape.

She waited for what seemed like forever. All she could hear was Madeline pressing up (and down). Then, just as she was about to give up, she heard:

"I say Mad, why don't! You sing while you? Are exercising!!!" It was the Second Year, earning his money. He sounded like a robot. Still, what could she expect for 5p? Dustin Hoffman? (He would have done it, but he was busy.) Still, at least she had the tape, even if she did drop it in a puddle gathering it together. All she had to do was give the tape to Bonnie and Clyde, and they would make her famous . . . wouldn't they?

THE SHOW MUST GO ON

Yes. They would. And they did.

I know it seems impossible. But they had the Midas touch. Since the start of term, they had already opened a shop, and that had been expanded twice (once a week!). Getting Germ into the Pop Charts was simple. Getting her on *Top of the Pops* was simple. Getting her on *Going Live*, *On the Waterfront*, *UP2U*, *7T3*, *Get Fresh*, *Wired*, and *Network Seven* was simple. *Wogan* was a piece of cake. *Bob Says Opportunity Knocks* proved impossible. What *was* his problem?

If only Bonnie and Clyde had been approached to help with the fund-raising, they might have prevented it being a total disaster. What small amount of money had been raised had been eaten by Yob.

The big mistake they had made had been trying to raise money from within the school. No one in the school had any. Even William and Harry, whose family seemed to own half of the Known World, had empty pockets. They had even tried to get money out of the teachers, which just goes to show how desperate things got!

Peanut was addressing an emergency meeting, as Germ, Bonnie and Clyde arrived at school, after Germ's appearance on TV-AM.

"All I've got to say is: Path-et-flippin-ic!" Peanut was saying as they opened the classroom door. "What we need is a really good money-making scheme—"

"Did someone say 'what we need is a really good money-making scheme'?" cut in Bonnie.

"Erm . . . er . . . " said most of the class, who had not really been listening. But they were now.

"Look no further," Bonnie continued. "I am pleased to be able to announce that my latest discovery, Germ, the hottest pop sensation since George Michael—"

"Who?" questioned Quiff. Bonnie ignored him, and continued.

"Germ will be giving a concert, live, tonight, in aid of the School Fund. I've booked a television studio."

"Have you—?" Clyde started to say, but was silenced by a sharp kick to the left shin. "Ouch!" he concluded.

"Now, all you lot have got to do is sell tickets, tee-shirts, souvenir programmes, mugs, videos, albums, photos, etc. So, get cracking!" and with that Bonnie swept out, with Clyde limping after her.

A live concert! In front of live people! Germ couldn't believe it. Up until now she had been able to mime to the tape she'd made of Mad. Everyone had loved it. In fact, that had been her first surprise. When Germ listened to the tape, all she could hear was somebody singing a yucky song, while doing press-ups in a squelchy field. But the record company boss had read all sorts of things into it, and given them a ten-year contract there and then, on condition that they came up with more of the same sort of thing. The record had also been banned by Radio One, which had doubled its sales. She was now the most popular pop artist in Britain, if not the world. And, tonight, she would sing live.

Or rather, she wouldn't.

Because she couldn't.

And that was the problem.

She needed Nick's help. She went to look for him.

The television studio was fabulous, if a bit quiet, even for a Sunday. One or two of the Palace Hill pupils also found it odd that they all had to climb in through a window, but they accepted Clyde's assurance that this was a short-cut. They also found it odd that they had to take the front off the fusebox in order to get the power on. You would have thought that with all the millions of pounds worth of equipment available, the lights might have a more sophisticated way of being turned on — like a switch. PC told them that television cameras cost £50,000, and you don't even get a plug. Typical!

Anyway, they were in, and they started the business of getting ready for the concert. Peanut, Yob and Doughnut set up the souvenir stall.

"Do you think I look thinner?" Doughnut enquired of Peanut.

"Thinner than what?" Peanut asked.

Harry came up, carrying guitars and so forth. "If you ask me, the way we got into this place was very strange," he whispered to Peanut.

"Nobody did ask you."

They had just had their second tiff.

PC and Jimmy were erecting the sound equipment.

"All you have to do is join the two wires together," explained Jimmy.

"How do you know?" asked PC, who was less sure.

"I read it in *Biggles Joins The Two Wires Together*." Suddenly there was a blinding flash and, when the smoke cleared, it appeared that Jimmy had decided to lie down for a while, as described in *Biggles Lies Down For A While*.

A quartet of strangely clad musicians walked past William and Mandy.

"They're Germ's backing band, the Germaleenies," explained Mandy. "They're Fab and Gear apparently."

"Oh. What are the other two called?" William knew less about the pop scene than his father did.

So . . . everything was ready for Germ's Big Night. But where was Germ?

"So, you see, Nick, that's the problem." Germ had just got her problem off her pink gingham chest.

"Hmm," was Nick's immediate reaction. But, after thinking about it for a minute or two, he came up with: "Ah."

Quiff's reaction was far more positive. "What did you say again?"

Germ explained again. And again. And then once more for luck.

"Let's see if I've got this straight," pondered Nick. "You've got to sing, which you can't, cus you didn't, cus it was Mad, but Bonnie and Clyde don't know that, cus you haven't told them, cus you can't, cus you'll lose yer contract if they find out. Is that about it?"

"That's exactly about it, Nick," agreed Germ.

"What was the problem again?" asked Quiff.

"Leave it to us," Nick said.

"Yeah. We'll sort it out," assured Quiff. "What's up, exactly, Nick?"

"We've got to find Mad. Come on." So saying, Nick left.

"Right. That should be easy enough," said Quiff, following his leader. "I thought you said that Germ had a *real* problem. Having to find Mad doesn't seem too much of one to me." It was just as well that Quiff was only the brawn, really, contemplated Nick, as they both headed backstage.

"Front of House", as they say in theatreland, the audience was arriving. They had all paid £50 a seat. After all, it was for charity. They would all be stung for much more before the night was over, as they shelled out for the album of the concert, the video of the album of the concert, the tee-shirt of the video of the album of the concert, and the mug. But they didn't know that yet. They smiled and chattered cheerfully, as they gave their tickets to Yob at the window, who tore and ate one half, allowing them to retain the other half (to eat later, if they so wished). There were, naturally, a few local dignitaries, such as the mayor and his lovely wife, and Mr Plunger, the tone-deaf school music teacher, plus his long-time companion, Ms Savage, the one-armed school pianist. There were also a smattering of local "Celebs" (as they say in Medialand): there was Tracy Stove, Miss Secondary Glazing five years running, accompanied by her father, B W Stove, managing director of Stove's Secondary Glazing PLC. Representing the local music scene was "Earwax" (real name Derek Froom), self-styled King of Punk, whose band The Rubbish had an enormous hit in the late-seventies with "If You Interrupt Me Once More When I'm Talking, I Will Get Really Cross, Probably", which was adopted as an anthem by strawberry farmers everywhere.

While the audience was buzzing Front of House, backstage things were hotting up.

Three of the Germaleenies were looking for someone who knew how to tune a guitar. The fourth Germaleeny was looking for someone who knew how to tune a drumstick. Nick and Quiff were looking for Mad. They found her, in one of the backstage dressing-rooms, getting dressed for the concert and after-show celebration party. She was that optimistic. She was wearing something that looked like it might have once belonged to Barbara Cartland.

"Hello, you chaps!" she greeted them. "I say, you don't think this is too racy for a popular concert, do you?"

"Nah," said Nick. "Listen. You've got to sing tonight instead of Germ."

But Mad wasn't really listening. She was far too busy sorting out her accessories. "If you like. I must find some jewellery."

"Cus, if you don't," Nick threatened, "you'll get this!" So saying, Nick waved a long, necklace-like worm in front of her face. Mad considered this: "Oh, I don't think so. It'll clash with my lipstick."

Not realizing that they were at cross purposes, Nick assumed that she was being difficult. "Going to be tricky, eh? Right! Quiff."

Quiff produced an enormous spider, which had once starred in his History of Robert the Bruce, the First Australian King of Scotland. Mad considered the spider.

"It's better, but it's still not really me, somehow. You haven't anything in green, have you?"

Nick was near boiling point. He pulled out his pet frog. "This is your last chance. Sing tonight, or . . ."

Mad saw the frog. "Perfect!" said Mad.

"Rivet!" said the frog, and it jumped straight down Mad's throat.

"Ugg-ugger-ugg!" said Mad.

"That's torn it! said Quiff. "How's she going to

sing with a frog in her throat?"

The simple answer was, of course, that she wasn't. But Germ, standing in the wings, did not know this. Bonnie and Clyde, sitting in the studio control box, where they were supervising the recording of the video, were unaware of it too.

The Germaleenies, who were now playing the introduction to Germ's Hit Single, knew nothing about it. They didn't know much about playing the introduction to Germ's Hit Single, either.

Nick, Quiff, Mad and the frog arrived in the wings.

"Mad can't sing!" explained Nick.

"She's got to!" panicked Germ. She shook Mad. "You must sing for me! Now!"

"Don't jump down her throat!" said Nick.

"The frog's already done that," pointed out Quiff.

"Ugg-ugger-ugg," said Mad.

"Rivet," replied the frog.

"What on earth's going on? yelled Bonnie, in the control box.

"You can do it," said Nick, giving Germ a push.

She couldn't. She stood in the middle of the stage, in front of the microphone, with the talking-into bit pointing at her, and froze, even though it was boiling hot under the lights.

She stood there, rigid with fear, for what seemed like years. The Managing Director of Stove's Secondary Glazing PLC timed it with his (fake) Rolex, which he held high above his head so that it caught the light, and the envious eyes of everyone else in the auditorium. If only they'd known it was a fake! But they'd still have wanted one.

The concert could have ended in disaster, but for Mandy, standing in the wings, watching: "I may be boring," she murmured quietly, "but I've got to save the day!"

And she did. She took the place by storm. Years of going on three-day coach trips to the Rhine, the Amsterdam Tulip Festival, and Bruges Chocolate-Eating (and Being Sick) Festival had taught her a fund of sing-along songs, and she soon had the audience Packing Up Their Troubles In Their Old Kitbags, and letting the world know that it was A Long Way To Tipperary. In fact, the audience all agreed, as they climbed back out of the window with their arms full of videos, tee-shirts, albums, etc, that they hadn't had such a good time since the war. Earwax had enjoyed singing the songs so much that he contacted his ex-record company the very next day, and suggested cutting a come-back album, entitled: "Earwax And The Rubbish Sing The Songs From The Second World War Which Some Of The Older Folks Like My Mum and Dad And Auntie Are Still Singing You'd Be Amazed Really I Know I Was".

While Earwax's ex-record company was explaining, as nicely as possible, why he was being thrown out of their offices, the pupils of Palace Hill were congratulating themselves on the success of the concert. Not congratulating Mandy, you'll notice. Still, that's the price you pay for being boring.

They stood staring at the mountain of money

that Bonnie and Clyde were in the middle of counting.

"It's vast!"

"It's bigger than Doughnut!"

"That's because Doughnut is getting smaller," pointed out Mandy, though no one was listening.

"We should get it all safely in the bank," suggested Harry, and they all started to gather it together.

"Not so fast!" said Bonnie, calmly but very firmly. Firmly enough to stop them in their tracks. "As concert promoter, Clyde and I have to take our cut."

"Well, yes, of course, but . . . " began Harry.

"Then there's overheads, underheads, discount, datcount, surtax, income tax, outcome tax, vat tax, pole tax, brass tax, tin tax . . . "

"OK! OK!" cut in Peanut. "So, how much is left?"

"This much," said Bonnie, handing her a single coin.

"This won't even buy a pencil!" exclaimed Peanut, looking at the coin disgustedly.

"Oh, it will," said Clyde. "We've got a very nice pencil on Special Offer at the moment. You can just about afford it!"

And they scooped up the money and were gone.

LOCAL HERO

One good thing had come out of the fund-raising. Two, if you count the mega-store that Bonnie and Clyde were currently having built behind the bike sheds. The One Good Thing was Doughnut. His Sponsored Diet may not have raised any money, but it had worked in every other way.

He was now thin. More than that, he was lean, scanty, slender, spare, sparse, flimsy, sylph-like, gossamer.

He could certainly not be called fat any more.

And, with this new-found thinness came a new-found popularity. He was suddenly in demand. Oh, he had always been popular in a sort of "Good Old Doughnut" sort of way. But now, girls fancied him! He got mobbed. He got followed. He got slipped notes. He got winked at. He got his bottom pinched (those that could find it). He loved it!

One of the casualties of the fund-raising had been Germ. Gone was the fame. Gone was the fortune. Gone was the pink gingham. That was the only bit she wasn't sorry about. But it was all over. Her bright star had turned back into a pumpkin. At least she was now safely back in Nick's Gang, being mistaken for a bloke.

Another casualty was Harry. One could safely say that the Romance of the Year was now the Joke of the Week. Harry confided in his elder brother: "Oh, sibling. I think I'm losing her!"

"Forget her," advised the older, sadder and wiser William. He had been down this particular road himself, and discovered it was all cobbles. He was also preoccupied with his own future. "One wishes one was old enough to shave," he said.

"Why?" queried his younger brother.

"One wouldn't bother. Stubble would suit one's descent into yobbery." William had made a decision. He would seek out Nick Knuckle.

The Second Good thing to come out of the fund-raising, as I mentioned earlier (you don't remember? Oh, come on, it was only on the last page. Do you want me to wait while you check? OK, but don't be long) was the financial reward for Bonnie and Clyde, who were currently planning their next venture. (Ah! You're back! Sorry, I carried on. I got tired of waiting.)

"Clyde," said Bonnie.

"Yes, Bonnie?" said Clyde.

"You know how everyone at Palace Hill always

fancies someone else?"

"Yes, Bonnie."

"Clyde. Do you fancy me?"

"What year is it?"

"1988."

"No, Bonnie. I don't fancy you for another four years. Just in time to make our first fortune."

"That's a relief," sighed Bonnie. "What about making a blockbusting film that clears millions at the box office, Clyde?"

"That's a good idea, Bonnie."

And so they did.

"Listen, Nick. One wants to join your gang," said William, when he finally tracked down the bully, behind the lavs, cheating at marbles.

"Eh!" exclaimed Quiff and Germ, reacting to William (they didn't notice the cheating).

"Sssh!" Nick held up his hand for silence, then realized that it was him going "Sssh!".

"It's not that simple," said Nick to William. "There's a test."

"Oh. Can it be sums? One's quite good at those."

"It's photography."

"Oh, goody!" William was fairly good at that, as he had an uncle "in the trade", as they said in Photographyland.

Nick then produced an extremely large camera from his extremely small jacket, which he'd had since he was extremely small, and handed it to William.

"What do you want one to snap? Wildlife?"

"That's right," smirked Nick. "The staffroom,

at lunchtime!"

William gulped.

The Rest of the School did more than that when they auditioned for parts in the film. They gulped, swallowed, gargled, rolled their eyes, stood on one leg, removed one leg, pulled out all their hair — anything to get noticed.

"Come on! This is our big chance! He's talking about us again. He's going to write us into Bonnie's film!"

"Nah, he isn't! You wait and see. He'll get us all worked up, then it'll come to nothing."

"Well, I'm going to put extra make-up on, just in case."

"You're wasting your time."

"We'll see."

Yes, the Rest of the School did absolutely everything they could think of to get into the movie.

They needn't have bothered.

What did I tell you?"

"It's going to be a blockbuster," said Clyde, at the Press conference, called to launch the start of shooting. "I've signed up Doughnut as the lead."

"Doughnut? You mean the Fat Boy?"

"The newly slim and ultra cool boy," corrected Clyde. "Actually, we're thinking of changing his name from Doughnut to Iced Finger."

"Who's going to be the female lead?" asked the Cinema and Indoor Bowls Critic from the local free newspaper.

"Peanut."

"*Peanut!!!*"

"Yes. She didn't even have to audition. I found her in the street. Beating up a lamp-post."

Green smoke swirled. Hot geysers shot from the earth. The heat of seven suns blazed down on the barren land. An heroic figure strode into view. In his hand, his trusty sword. On his arm, his beloved Princess.

"Oh, Crud the Barbarian," purred the Princess. "You are truly awesome."

"You ain't so bad yourself, Princess Towanny-wanny," growled Crud.

"But no man, however hunky, has ever entered the Ju-Ju zone and returned," she pleaded.

"Maybe they like it there." He was *so* laid-back!

"Listen. My mother was a Ju-Ju mutant."

Crud paused to consider this. As he did so, the green smoke cleared, revealing the Second-Year Pole-Vault Team getting in some much-needed practice.

"Cut! Cut!" yelled PC from behind the camera. "Where's the green smoke? Who's on the green smoke?"

"Who's Green Smoke Monitor?" snapped Bonnie.

"One is," sulked Harry, who was lucky to be involved in the film at all.

"You're fired!" barked Bonnie. Oh, well. He wasn't even that lucky any more!

"You can be teaboy," she relented. Now, that *was* lucky.

"Can't one be Champagne boy?" Don't push

your luck, Harry!

William wasn't having a great deal of luck either.

"Why has Mr Grunter got his feet in the soup?" asked Quiff, as they studied the photograph that William had just risked his life to take in the staffroom.

"Never mind that. Is one in the gang?" begged William.

"Ah, well, that's Part A of the test," explained Nick. "Part B is to take this bone and give it to Mr Blatherwick's Doberman, Elliott."

"Give a bone to Elliott? Simple!"

"Then take it back again!"

GULP!

During a break in filming, while an army of technicians were working out how to get the lens-cap off the camera, Mandy — the Unit Make-up Girl — was mopping Crud's brow. She was also chatting to the star: "You're ever so good in this, Doughnut. Funny, I've known you all my life. You were the boy next door, until you ate our house. I always thought of you as a Fat Friend. But, without all your blubber, you're beautiful. I wonder, if I ever lose my boringness, whether you'll think I'm beautiful."

Doughnut turned to speak to her as she went to powder his nose. She powdered his teeth and gums instead.

Princess Towanny-wanny, in the shape of Peanut, pushed her out of the way. "Clear off, you! I want to practise the kissing bit . . . I've learned that bit!"

As Peanut buried her face in Doughnut's stick-on beard, Harry watched and seethed. He would be revenged on Crud the Barbarian. And soon.

Madeline was just returning from her 75-mile morning run, when she came across the slumped and battered body of William.

"Why, Prince! You look as ragged as a rugger-scrum."

"One has just taken this bone from Elliott the Doberman!" spluttered William.

"You rotter, stealing a doggy-woggy's bone!"

"One didn't steal it! One exchanged it! For one of one's own!" replied William. Mad was confused.

"But why exchange bones with a bona-fide fido?"

"Simple. One is undertaking an initiation test for the Knuckle Gang. One has decided to join the moron-majority!"

It was tea-break time on the film set. Harry was handing out plastic cups of something that purported to be tea. He arrived in front of Doughnut.

"Tea . . . milk . . . sugar?" Harry asked, sticking on his sickliest smile.

"Not for me, Guvner, I don't want to put any weight back on."

"Are you stupid or something?" snapped Clyde. "D' you want him to be a fat slob again, and ruin the film?"

"Of course not! Sorry!" lied Harry. He had an idea.

Doughnut turned his attention to Mandy. He had always liked her, but now . . . something inside him was stirring . . . it was confusing. But he knew what he must do.

"Mandy?"

"Yes, Doughnut?"

"D'you remember what you were saying earlier?"

"How much earlier? I remember mentioning that my sensible shoes that won't give me corns in later life needed new laces . . . was it that? Or was it me mentioning that the pork butcher in the High Street has changed his window display?"

"No! It was neither! It was . . . oh, Mandy . . . " He was about to tell her of the yearning in his heart, when Harry returned with a glass of clear liquid.

"Iced water, oh ex-lard mountain?" asked Harry, very, very, pleasantly.

"Iced water?" queried Doughnut.

"Certainly! It's what all the Big Stars drink. Honest!"

"Oh. Very well, then. Thanks." And he took the glass. The glass containing the water. The water containing the sugar cube. And he drank it.

SPPPPPPPPOOOOINNNNNNNNGGGG!!!

Doughnut put on seventeen stones four pounds and three ounces exactly.

"No!" said Doughnut. What else could you say? "I've put all my weight back on!" Yes. You could say that. "Now I'll never be able to tell her!" Doughnut continued.

"Tell who?" asked Mandy.

"I can't tell you!" moaned Doughnut.

"Tell me what?" Mandy was getting nowhere fast.

Harry danced for joy. "I did it! I spiked his drink! Now that he's fat again, Peanut will love me once more!"

Peanut took one look at Doughnut. "Wow! Great! Much, much more of what I liked before!"

"Brilliant!" enthused Bonnie. "A great ending to the film! Crud the Barbarian becomes a mutant like Princess Towanny-wanny, and they live happily ever after in the Ju-Ju Zone! Amazing! Places, everyone! And Action!"

Harry tasted the bitter fruits of rejection.

William couldn't taste anything. He had lost all his senses, and all feeling from his body. The parts of the initiation test, all twenty-six of them, had proved progressively more complicated. He had battled on valiantly, but fallen at the final fence. He would never be a member of Nick Knuckle's Gang. His dream was shattered.

Unless . . .

THE VISIT

There is an expression that goes, "If you can't join them, beat them". Although I think that's a slight mis-quote.

However, that's exactly what William had decided to do — beat them. And he chose the day of the overseas visit to do it.

Palace Hill Comprehensive School was to play host to a small group of students from a school in Dusseldorf, which is in Germany. Or, at least, it was the last time anyone checked. This was quite a treat for a school that had very few visitors. Oh, yes, there were the police two or three times a week. Or rather, two or three times a day. Then there were the social workers and the probation officers; the people from the Department of Health to check whether the school had become a health hazard yet; members of the local professional football team, asking for their ball back; lollipop ladies asking for their lollipops back; ex-pupils who were stuck on the *Sun* crossword. But no one as important as an overseas visitor. So, as you can imagine, the school was buzzing with activity, as were the flies around the school bins.

Banners were erected bearing the legend "Welcome to the Germans", which says it all, really. They were made during the last war by an opportunist pessimist. He thought we would lose, and wanted to make the most out of it. They also put up bunting. (That's a strange word, isn't it? Bunting. It means a string of flags. Who had the idea to call a string of flags "bunting"? It's also a type of small bird. Perhaps, in ancient times, they celebrated the arrival of guests by hanging up a string of small birds, in much the same way as they killed the Fatted Calf in Biblical Times. It's not impossible. Where was I? Ah, yes! Bunting!)

They decorated the playground, the school gates, and themselves. Someone had the bright idea of all dressing in some form of Tyrolean dress — shorts and little hats with feathers for the boys, wide skirts and fancy aprons for the girls. Naturally, all that most of the boys could afford to do was cut their second-best school trousers (or even their only pair of school trousers) off at the knee. Only Harry had actually splashed out and bought a special pair of Leiderhosen, which is German for leather trousers. They were specially made for him by Harrods. He looked magnificent. He sounded decidely rude. I don't know if you've ever sat on a brand new leather sofa, but new leather does tend to make little squeaky noises which sound like . . . well . . .

they sound as though they are not being made by the leather. Do you follow? Or shall I draw a diagram?

Anyway, everyone was busily preparing the playground for the arrival of the German visitors. Peanut, as Form Representative, was "supervising", which is the correct term for "letting everyone else do the dirty work". Yob was with her, of course, but it was a strangely changed Yob.

"Das Armband ist gerissen . . . I have got a broken strap . . . Das Armband ist gerissen . . . " said Yob, by opening his mouth, but without moving his lips.

"What's up with him?" Peanut demanded of Mandy, who was still around, even though Peanut and Harry were very much an ex-item.

"I've been teaching him German," explained a slightly embarrassed Mandy. "I lent him a German language tape, and he swallowed it."

"Dieses Bettlaken ist schmutzig . . . this sheet is dirty," said the tape inside Yob, just to confirm Mandy's story.

"You must give me the recipe," commented Doughnut, who had now fully recovered his appetite.

Peanut sighed and continued her tour of inspection, which took her past Mad, who was pinning a copy of the day's schedule to the wall.

"Ten hundred hours: arrival of Germans. Welcoming Committee standing by," she read aloud, then suddenly realized . . . oh, no! How embarrassing! The Welcoming Committee consisted of Peanut (as Form Rep) and Harry (as

Token Royal). Harry and Peanut! They were
hardly talking to each other! How very
embarrassing! Well, it was too late to do
anything. Oh, if only they had thought in time,
they could have switched Harry for William.
After all, William should really be the Token
Royal, as he was the oldest. Although at the
moment, he was the *oddest* as well. Poor
William! All this Mad thought but did not say, as
Bertolt Brecht would put it. (I thought I'd
mention that, as Brecht was a famous German
playwright.)

By the way, if you are reading this book in bed,
under the covers by torchlight, now would be a
good time to get ready to hold your torch between
your teeth, so that you've got both hands free to
turn the page. If you haven't got any teeth, grip
the torch under your chin. Or, if you're double-
jointed, grip the torch between your feet, behind
your head. If you want to try turning the page
with your torch in your teeth, feet, or anywhere
else you can think of, I really don't mind waiting,
as long as you're not too long. I'll practise writing
under the covers while you're gone. See you in a
second or two.

leth'ssee. thiusisnot aseasy asn ut seens,
obcviously.

No. I'll give that a miss, I think.

Ah! You're back. Good. I missed you.

As I was saying, in the opinion of Mad, and
indeed most of the others, William was becoming
decidedly odd. Take today, for example. He was
not in Tyrolean dress, as were all the others. Oh,
no! He was dressed as a Punk! Harry could not

help but notice this, as he squeaked up to his elder brother. (Oh, sorry, I've gone over the page without warning you. Hope you haven't dropped your torch.) He also couldn't help but notice that William was learning to speak German.

"Do you want a bunch of fives . . . Brauchen Sie ein, er, Bunch of Funfs," William was saying as Harry squeaked alongside. And, as Harry arrived, William observed, "Been on the prunes, have you, Windy?"

Bit Rude. Very unlike William. Harry winced.

"No, actually," he explained. "It's these leather trousers. They're new. Anyway, you can talk! You look like the cover of Mother's Gary Glitter album. Why such patent plebbery?"

"Well, don't tell a soul," confided William. "But one intends to take over Nick Knuckle's Gang!"

Harry could not believe his ears. He also couldn't believe William's ears, which looked larger than ever under the punk hairstyle.

"YOU INTEND TO TAKE OVER NICK KNUCKLE'S GANG!" exclaimed Harry, in shock. "Don't worry, I won't tell a soul."

"Neither will we," said everyone within a ten-mile radius. Harry had just broadcast the information over the public address system set up to welcome the Germans.

So that was what it was all about — the punk gear, the moodiness — it started to fall into place. If you can't join them, beat them.

Nick, who amazingly had not heard Harry broadcast William's intentions, now ran through the school gates. He and his gang (well, it was still *his* gang at the moment!) had been on the look-out for the German coach. And they had just spotted it coming along the road. It had taken them by surprise, as they had been expecting a German coach — Horse Sprung Dung Technik. What they didn't know was that a local coach firm had been hired to collect the visitors from the airport and bring them to the school. It was the name on the side of the coach that made the Knuckle Gang think it was the right one: "GERRY'S COACH TOURS LIMITED".

"That'll be the one," said Nick to Quiff and Germ. And, for once, he was right.

"The Gerrys are coming!" yelled Nick, rushing to join the rest of the school, who were all lined up to greet their visitors.

The sight that greeted the Germans as they filed off the coach in their designer clothes was bizarre to say the very least: rows of English schoolchildren dressed in homemade Tyrolean costume, and waving Union Jacks. The Germans wanted to ask "What's going on here then?", but they didn't because (A) they were too polite, and (B) they spoke absolutely no English.

If the visitors found their first sight of their English hosts alarming, the next few hours were mind-blowing.

Peanut put on her friendliest smile, and made a little speech of welcome in her best bedside manner. This caused three of the Germans to cry, and one to rush and lock himself in the coach. There then followed a demonstration of English school-life, organized by Ms Wren-Stamper, who had phoned in sick that morning.

Then there was a display of English Country Dancing, which looked very odd in Tyrolean costume.

Form 3F, who were not destined to become captains of industry, airline pilots or even transplant surgeons, played "Greensleeves" on their recorders. At least, that's what the majority of people thought it sounded most like. None of the actual players seemed to know what it was called, as they were playing from memory.

The Drama Club performed "The Rhyme Of The Ancient Mariner", in mime, and in its entirety. Mandy had a very small part in this, as a Mackerel. She was very good. The Albatross itself had been made by Form 4C in Woodwork. Unfortunately it crashed on its maiden flight in the opening stanza, but Doughnut saved the day by standing in, wearing a cardboard beak.

As soon as news leaked that the Drama Club were taking part in the Opening Ceremony, all the school's other clubs insisted that they, too, must take part. Consequently:

The Under Thirteen's Freestyle Karate Club gave a demonstration of Various Silly Ways Of Breaking A House Brick. As a finale, Tiggy Merkin, the Club's star pupil, demonstrated the Flying Leap To Break A Roofing Tile With The Side Of The Foot. Unfortunately, he overdid the run-up, missed the tile, and demolished most of the Science block.

The Fifth Form Chess Club demonstrated Illegal Castling.

The School Swimming Club gave an

interesting demonstration of Syncronized Swimming. What made it particularly interesting was the fact that it was performed on dry land, since the school swimming pool was nowhere near the playground, and anyway it had been commandeered by Mr Strangler's "Save the Whale" campaign.

After further demonstrations of Macramé, Knitting, Juggling, Netball, Football, Meditation, Cookery, Scrabble and Gymnastics, the Opening Ceremony, which had over-run by three hours, was finally brought to a close with the singing of the German National Anthem. Strangely, none of the Germans joined in. It later transpired that they hadn't recognized it.

Was it this, or was it the inscription on the side of the coach, that caused Jimmy's confusion? Whatever it was, it did not help the day to become a resounding success. Sitting in his air-raid shelter, Jimmy could vaguely hear the strains of "Deuschland, Deuschland, Uber Alles". He quickly pushed up his homemade periscope, and scanned the horizon. He focused on the side of the coach, and read to his horror "GERRY'S COACH TOURS LIMITED".

"Oh, no!" he exclaimed. "I think the Gerries have invaded, as described in *Biggles Thinks The Gerries Have Invaded!*" He turned to his trusty fish."

"Monty! Winston! This calls for some serious action! I didn't think they'd come by coach, though, somehow! Jolly cunning, the Boche!" Jimmy put himself, and the fish, on "Battle Alert", and started to don his battle fatigues.

Jimmy's mistake would prove to be a great embarrassment to the pupils at Palace Hill. The visit was a cultural exchange, and had nothing whatever to do with anything that had happened in the past between the two countries. In fact, all mention of the war had been strictly taboo. The School's Formation Ballroom Dancing Club had been made to scrap their plans to perform the Battle of Britain as a Bossa Nova. Their mothers were furious when they found out. They had been up half the night, sewing sequinned swastikas on the back of their offspring's ballgowns.

To add to the embarrassment, Harry and Peanut who were barely being civil to each other, were now giving the Germans a conducted tour of the school, much of which was out of bounds, as it was waiting to be condemned.

Harry's trousers were still squeaking rather badly, which the Germans naturally assumed was something completely different, but were too polite to laugh. Yob still had the tape inside him.

"Ist dies Trinkwasser?" said Yob's tape, causing the Germans to look very confused. They were in the corridor, outside the video room.

"This is the video room," said Harry, very loudly to cover the squeaks from his trousers. Peanut simply smirked, which annoyed Harry.

"One can show them around the school on one's own, you know," he told her. "One won't get lost!"

"I wish one would!" she replied. Fortunately, the Germans couldn't understand, but they could have cut the atmosphere with a knife, had any of them been carrying one.

Inside the video room, Quiff had just sat on PC's computer keyboard, causing it to behave very oddly. Almost as oddly as William, who was somewhere else, plotting his take-over.

"Oh, Quiff! You've babbled my Qwerty!" exclaimed PC, just after he'd done it.

"Oh, no! I've mucked up your computer as well."

"That's what I meant!"

"Was it?" Quiff would never be able to talk computer language.

"This is the video room," said Harry again, as he squeakily led his party of Germans into PC's inner sanctum.

"Not now, Harry, please! I've got to get debugging!"

"Oh, sorry! Back everybody!"

It is not easy to reverse a large party of people who are still entering a very small space. It is even more difficult if that large group of people speak no English at all, and are also trying to control themselves because they think you've got wind. Harry, somehow, managed it.

Quiff got scooped up by the party of Germans, leaving PC alone to sort out her computer. According to the message on the screen, it appeared that somehow she had become patched into the School's mainframe computer. She didn't even know that the school had one. Further exploration revealed that this computer controlled all the school's facilities: lighting, heating, plumbing, meals, lessons, etc. PC patched into the plumbing, just to see what happened!

"And these are the school lavatories," Harry was telling a group of totally nonplussed Germans, who were all crammed into a very inconvenient space. Unfortunately, for various reasons, the lavs were about the only place available to be toured.

It was while they were in there that PC patched into the plumbing.

The water from the WC bowls cascaded over the tops of the cubicle doors, and landed, like a waterfall on to the brand new designer clothes of the visitors.

Unaware of what she had done, PC decided that she must locate the school computer, in order to sort out the muddle that Quiff had caused. This she now set about doing.

After buying new clothes from Bonnie and Clyde's mega-store, the visitors sat down to a Specially Prepared School Meal. Rumours that went around later were untrue. The meal did not make *all* of the Germans sick. Only most of them.

The Palace Hill pupils, who knew better than to eat school meals, were in a nearby field, preparing for the highlight of the afternoon, the Anglo-German Fun Run.

Nick, Quiff and Germ were dressed from head to foot in red, white and blue, and were behaving like football supporters.

"Oh, really, Nick! You're supposed to be the Race Marshall. You're supposed to be impartial!" complained Mad, who was part of the

English team.

"I am an Impartial Marshall, aren't I lads?" said Nick.

"Course you are!" agreed Quiff and Germ, and all three of them then launched into yet another chorus of "You'll Never Walk Alone".

The English Team consisted of Mandy, Mad, Doughnut and Harry. William was to have run, but, since he had turned punk, the chains on his legs made it difficult even to walk. Besides, he was behind a tree, plotting. Everyone knew he was there, except Nick. They all also knew what he was plotting, except Nick. They just naturally assumed that he'd never pull it off.

Nobody, however, knew that lurking behind another tree they would find Jimmy, in full battle dress and ready to save his country from the tyranny of the jackboot, as described in *Biggles Saves His Country From The Tyranny Of The Jackboot.*

Peanut had elected to support the Germans, partly as a Friendly Gesture, but mostly to put herself on the opposite side to Harry. Harry, by the way, was no longer squeaking, you'll be pleased to hear.

"Now, don't forget what we agreed, chaps," Mad was instructing her team.

"No. Of course not," agreed Doughnut. "What was it?"

"FHB" said Mad, with a sigh.

"Oh, yes. Of course," remembered Doughnut. "What does that mean?"

"Family Hold Back," explained Mad. "In this case, we are Family. The Germans are our guests.

Therefore we must let them win."

"Oh. Right," agreed Doughnut, who was a bad loser.

"Where are they, anyway?" said Harry, who was itching to get going.

Cheers from Peanut, and boos from the Knuckle Gang told them that the Germans were approaching. All three of them. Bonnie and Clyde were with them, and were able to explain the situation to the others. Clyde spoke pidgin German, parrot fashion. Or at least well enough to sell the Germans some very expensive running gear. And do a sponsorship deal with them, which meant that the Germans were now covered from head to foot in adverts for "Bonnie and Clyde PLC". He had also managed to ascertain that the Specially Prepared School Meal had laid low the German star runner, which left the German team one short.

"One of you must run for the Germans," instructed Mad, who wanted everything very fair.

"Germ can do it," said Nick. "She's already half way there, cus she's a Germ!"

"Yeah, I might be a Germ, but I'm not a Man."

"Aren't yer?" said Quiff, genuinely surprised. She still hit him.

"Nick can do it." The voice came from behind a tree.

"Who says?" asked Nick. He had never been any good at recognizing voices (or trees).

"One says." William stepped, with difficulty, from behind the tree. He moved, as menacingly as his leg chains would allow, towards Nick. The effect was rather like Clint Eastwood in a sack-race. He had been biding his time, and this was it.

"Why me?"

"Because," replied William Eastwood, "One says so, cloth-head."

"Yeah? Well, that's not good enough," pointed out Nick. "Such arbitary action flies in the face of a democratic electoral process."

"Alright," said William. "We'll stick your name in a hat."

"That's more like it," agreed Nick.

"Anyone got a hat to put Nick's name in?"

"Use mine," suggested Nick. "It's already got my name in it."

"Thanks." William took Nick's hat, gave it a shake, then ripped the name-tag from the lining. He handed it to Nick.

"There. What does it say?"

"Nick Knuckle," read Nick Knuckle, with some difficulty.

"There," said William. "You have been democratically elected to run for the German team."

"That's fair enough," agreed Nick. Then Bonnie and Clyde sold him a complete set of designer sportswear.

"On your marks," called Peanut. "Get set! Go!"

Thus, the race was started, and the first stage of William's plot was under way. The runners were not to know what awaited them, further along the route.

"Right. Now to nobble the nasties, as described in *Biggles Nobbles The Nasties*," muttered Jimmy, to no one in particular.

"This super-duper Diversion Ploy should do it!"

He placed a signpost in the ground. The crosspiece of the signpost read "THIS WAY" in one direction, and "NOT THIS WAY" in the other. The idea was to get the Germans to run the wrong way. He couldn't wait to see if it worked. He didn't have long to wait, as the first German soon came into view.

"Hide!" he told himself, and did so.

The first German ran straight past the sign without giving it a second look. Once he had gone, Jimmy reappeared from his hiding place, and pulled the crosspiece off the signpost, throwing it into the air in disgust.

"That wasn't very successful! Oh, well. Back to the drawing board." And he left. Had he stayed around slightly longer, he would have witnessed the second German runner travelling from north to south, only to be met by the flying piece of signpost, travelling from east to west. The signpost struck the German on the side of the head. The signpost then went north, and the German's chances of winning the race went west.

Meanwhile, PC's search for the school mainframe computer was still continuing. The cursor on her screen was travelling from right to left, and was currently searching near the staff room, and it seemed it was getting warmer . . .

"Brilliant," said an ever-optimistic Jimmy, as he put the finishing touches to his latest trap.

"A trip-wire-activated-spring-loaded-boxing-glove-trap. Let's see: the victim comes along, trips on the trip-wire, which activates the boxing glove, fitted to a spring inside the hastily cut trap-door in the side of this tree. I do hope the conservationists don't mind; it is for a good cause!" He then heard the approaching German.

"Ah! Sounds like an approaching German! Hide!" And he did.

Well, the German did all he should have done, but the trap did not fire. Once the German had passed, Jimmy came out of hiding.

"Hopeless!" he exclaimed, tugging at the trip-wire.

"Useless!" he reiterated, tugging at the trip-wire and glaring at the trap-door in the tree.

"Pathetic!" he complained, as he hit the trap-door with his fist, then bent over to tug at the trip-wire, thus avoiding the boxing glove that now flew out of the tree at three hundred miles an hour, straight past Jimmy, and straight into the face of a passing German, who was laid out flat, unnoticed by Jimmy.

"Oh, well," complained Jimmy, "back to the drawing board!"

The cursor of PC's computer was now outside the Headmaster's study. It had stopped. Could this mean that the school computer was located inside the Head's study? It could be. PC had never been in there. Come to think of it, she didn't know a single person who had! It was time to investigate!

"Just the ticket," said Jimmy, as he placed the

inviting glass of water on to the small round table.

"Not an ordinary glass of water. But a glass of water liberally laced with quick-setting cement! Now, Friend Gerry comes along, sees the glass of water, 'Ah! A glass of water!' he says, in German. 'I'll drink that!' he says, in German. He drinks it, in German. The cement sets, *in* the German, and he goes rigid and nobbled. Brilliant! Hide!"

He dived behind the bush, thinking that the sound he had heard was an approaching German. He turned back to see the trap work, only to see a Greater-Crested Grebe drinking the glass of water. He tried to shoo the bird away, but too late! All the water was drunk, and the bird went rigid!

"Oh, well. Back to the drawing board!" So saying he threw the bird high into the sky, and left.

Shortly after he left, the third German arrived, very thirsty. He picked up the glass. It was empty. He looked very disappointed. He wondered where he could get a glass of water.

Just then, something struck him. It wasn't an idea for obtaining a drink. It wasn't even a glass full of water. It was a Greater-Crested Grebe, full of cement. He no longer needed a drink of water. He, like his other two companions needed an ambulance.

Ironically, Nick Knuckle, who wasn't a real German at all, was the only member of the German team still in the race. He now headed towards the finishing line, ahead of the field.

At the finishing line, Bonnie and Clyde were taking a few last-minute bets. Bonnie called out the odds:

"Place your bets now! Evens the favourites, Great Britain! Hundred to one the Germans! Roll up!"

"What's a hundred to one?" asked Germ, who didn't understand betting.

"It means," explained Clyde, who could tell a potential customer when he saw one, "that if you bet one pound, and win, I will give you a hundred pounds back."

"Cor," marvelled Germ.

"Yeah," said Quiff. "I've had a million pounds to win on the Germans. Cus Mad said the Germans must win, so that means I'll win, and I'll get a hundred times a million, which is a Trillibillion, or something."

"Oh, right!" said Germ. "I'll have a million pounds on the Germans, as well."

The bet had barely been placed, when Nick appeared around a blind corner, streets ahead of the field, heading straight for the line.

Germ and Quiff could see that all that money was nearly theirs. They could see an end to their lives of poverty. They could see a start to a life of luxury and spend, spend, spend! What they couldn't see was Jimmy, behind a tree, preparing to blow up what he believed to be the last bit of the German Invasion Force. Nick didn't see Jimmy, either. Nor did he see the explosives. But he felt them.

As the force of the blast blew him high into the sky, he looked down and saw the English team cross the finishing line. What he didn't see was the alien spacecraft orbitting the Earth above him.

But they saw him.

"Fbd!, jn. kugc*zs!" they said, which very roughly translates as "Not again!", and they headed back to the Planet Xfred&bvuypo *lerfes#, in the galaxy of Kent, at Warp Factor 876, which is very, very quickly. Neither did Nick see the Germans being taken to hospital, nor the ambulance waiting for him to return to earth, nor William stealing his gang.

"So, let's get this straight," Quiff was saying to Bonnie. "Germ and me both owe you a million pounds?"

"Each," said Clyde, who was greedy.

"Yes, but don't worry about paying now," smiled Bonnie. "We'll send the boys round for it, tomorrow!" Tomorrow! That didn't even give them time to skip the country. They were both feeling very sick. William saw this and moved in.

"Just a moment," said William. "One happens to be starting a gang, and anyone who joins one's gang today can take advantage of a very special offer. Each new recruit will get a million pounds. Oh, and a badge, of course." Well, he didn't have to say it twice! Quiff and Germ jumped at the opportunity!

"What! I'll join! Yeah!" yelled a greatly relieved Quiff.

"Yeah! Me too!" agreed Germ. "What's this badge like, exactly?"

And so the former Knuckle Gang, now the Windsor Gang, headed off, following their leader, and chanting his praises. Well, Quiff was, anyway. Germ was preoccupied.

"This badge . . . it's not pink, is it? Only I

really hate pink. Can it be black, with real blood splashes on it, that kind of stuff . . . ?"

And off they went into the sunset.

PC, meanwhile, was about to go into the Head's study. She turned the doorknob. She opened the door, and went in.

The sight that greeted her totally blew her motherboard.

That is to say: her mind.

14

WHERE CAROL-SINGERS DARE

The festival season was almost upon the inmates of Palace Hill.

Christmas. A time of giving and receiving.

It's also a time every school window in the country is covered in cotton-wool balls. It's meant to be snow. Snow!

Put your hands up if you remember snow. Three of you. I thought so. Because, if you remembered snow, you'd know it doesn't land on the *inside* of windows.

The pupils of Palace Hill didn't care. They stuck the cotton-wool on the windows. They also hung milk bottle tops, on the ends of bits of string, from the classroom ceiling. These were meant to represent . . . er . . . milk bottle tops on the ends of bits of string.

"What is going to happen to all that milk?" asked William, who was holding the ladder for Mad, who was hanging her five hundredth milk bottle top from the ceiling. Mad cast an eye over the eight crates of milk, festering in the corner of the room.

"Cheese", said Mad. And William smiled. Being a Royal, he was conditioned to do that. And he was feeling Royal again. Gone were the moods. Gone were the punk trappings. Gone, too, was the gang. Mad approved.

"I'm glad to see that you're more Princely than Punk these days, little Willy. And that you've given up gangs."

"Hm," said William. He hadn't the heart to admit that the gang had given up him.

In the corner of the classroom, the ex-Windsor Gang, now the Knuckle Gang, were throwing darts into a picture of Father Christmas. Nick threw a dart: "Santa's nose . . . 20 points." He threw another.

"Santa's bum . . . 19 points." He threw his third dart.

"Santa's bum again . . . a double bottom."

The gentle sobbing in one corner was coming from Mandy. "I love Christmas! It always makes me cry!"

"Oh," said Doughnut. "Is your Mum coming to the carol concert this morning?"

"Yes, it'll cheer her up. She loves carols. They make her cry."

But what of PC? I mean, in the last chapter she had her motherboard completely blown. And then, when we turn over the page, it's as if it never happened. Do we have such lack of concern for her?

And what did she see that caused her to blow her mind?

I'll tell you. She traced the school's mainframe computer to the Head's study. She had never been inside the Head's study. In fact, she didn't know anyone who had. She had never even *seen* the Head, although that wasn't so surprising. But . . . Now she knew why.

The Head was a computer — a massive, flashing, sparking, jabbering computer, a megabrain, with more bytes than a pack of hungry wolves.

How long had PC stood there? Hours? Days? Weeks? Certainly long enough for the entire school to be decorated for Christmas. Certainly long enough for Nick to come out of hospital and take his gang back. Now she had only one thought in her head. She must tell the others. And that was where she was now heading.

The assorted parents of the assorted pupils were heading towards the front doors of the school. Bonnie and Clyde were there, checking off the names, and ripping off the punters.

"Name?" Bonnie enquired of a thin, rather boring-looking woman.

"Mrs Chunder. Mandy's mother." She turned to the elegantly dressed red-head beside her.

"What's your little Chubby called?"

"Oh, gosh! One doesn't actually have a little chubby at the school! Although . . . "She leant closer to confide in Mrs Chunder, "I have Beetroot's name down for some time in the dim and distant. No. I'm standing in. I've come to view the old nephew's warbling Noel, OK, Yah?"

Mrs Chunder suddenly realized where she had seen the red-headed person before. It was on a stamp. She felt very humble.

"Oh. OK . . . er . . . yah. Oooh, look! There's Joyce Doughnut. Cooee! Over here!" She yelled at the fat lady wedged in the door. "She'll have been to her weight-watchers' class. Fighting a losing battle, if you ask me." She nudged the red-headed person, then realized that she was not the thinnest red-headed person in the world, and blushed.

Mrs Doughnut wheezed up.

"Mrs Doughnut, this is the Duchess of York. Duchess of York, this is Mrs Doughnut," said Mandy's mum in her poshest voice.

"Very nice," said Mrs Doughnut.

"Super, Yah," replied the Duchess, graciously.

By now, the rest of the mums were arriving, including Mrs Quiff 'n Airy, and Germ's mum, and, of course, Mrs Knuckle-Tattoo with her husband, who was receiving his last-minute instructions.

"Just make sure you behave yourself this year," she was telling him. Then, in confidence to the Duchess of York: "Last year he broke wind, right in the middle of Silent Night!"

"Oh," was the best the Duchess could manage, off the cuff.

Back in the classroom, PC was about to break the news which would cause all the girls to look concerned, a couple of the boys to be silly at the back, and the School Bully to say: "I think it's stupid, and I don't see what it's got to do with me!"

"The Head's a computer!" said PC.

Immediately, all the girls looked concerned. William and Harry started prodding each other, and generally being very silly at the back of the class.

"I think it's stupid, and I don't see what it's got to do with me!" said Nick.

If things ran true to form, it would now be the turn of the girl whom all the staff really liked — whose destiny dictated that she would go through a bad patch in her third year, but pull her finger out in her fourth year, pass all her exams in her fifth year, go off to college in her sixth year to become a teacher, and then go back to school again — to say: "I think we should take a vote on it!"

"I think we should take a vote on it!" said Mandy.

"There isn't time! This is an unstable situation!" pointed out PC. "Supposing the school's electricity was suddenly increased by a millionfold, so boosting the Head's artificial intelligence by mega amounts!"

"Could that happen?" asked Mad.

"Sure," said PC. "If the school was struck by lightning."

"But that's a million to one chance," Nick said, as the school was struck by lightning.

"I think we've got trouble!" said Doughnut.

"Too right! Trouble indeed!" said a huge voice that came from nowhere. Well, no. Not nowhere. Everywhere. Now here, now there. Who was it?

"This is the Head speaking." Oh. That's who it was. "Watch!"

They watched. The room rocked as it was gripped in a surge of power. The crates of milk bottles suddenly exploded, showering milk everywhere, like a massive white fountain.

"Would you like me to run an errand for you, Sir?" asked Mandy, in an effort to placate him.

"Silence!" screamed the Head.

"Don't you talk to my girl like that!" This was Doughnut speaking. Mandy turned and stared at him. Was he saying what she thought he was saying? That depended on *what* she thought he was saying. Was it what he had tried to say, but hadn't been able to, just before he suddenly went fat again. It was. And it was what she wanted to hear. Oh, there was so much to catch up on. So much to say, like . . .

"I want revenge!"

No. Not that! Gentle, loving things, like . . .

"I want revenge!"

There it was again. It wasn't Mandy. It was the Head.

"Revenge for what you've done to my beautiful school!" Beautiful? That proved it. The Head was definitely deranged.

"But first on my list are those pathetic apologies for parents!"

"What? Not mummy and daddy!" cried Nick.

"You're not going to blow up my mum and dad after they've turned up to school in their best clothes!" said Peanut, defiantly.

"Yes. Can't they go home and change first?"

"I'm not going to blow them up," cackled the

139

Head. "I'm going to do something much nastier. I'm going to set them all an exam. And I'm not going to let them leave this school until they've passed it!" Yes. That was much worse. The entire room was stunned into silence. Only Quiff found his voice.

"This test, can it be on Blackburn Rovers 1944-45, second eleven tour of Belgium? Otherwise my mum's got no chance."

Unaware of their fate, the parents were currently forming a fairly orderly queue, at Santa's Super-Grotto: Proprietors: Bonnie and Clyde (who else?). They thought that, at £5 a head, the entrance fee was very reasonable, and Mr Knuckle was currently sitting on Santa's knee. Santa/Clyde was being crushed underneath.

"What would you like for Christmas, little boy?" he asked.

"Pancakes."

Further revels were halted by the interruption of the Head.

"Stand up! Stand up! This is your Head speaking! I have a little test for you!"

Mrs Quiff 'n Airy tried to point herself in the direction that she assumed the voice had come from.

"Can it be on Blackburn Rovers, 1944-45 second eleven tour of Belgium?"

Something had to be done. They couldn't allow their parents to be kept at the school until they had passed the exam. For some of them that would definitely mean the rest of their lives.

Imagine it! Your parents, stuck in the school for the rest of their lives! Who'd get your tea ready?

Going to school for the rest of your life. No one in their right mind would want to do that, would they? "Teachers do it," I hear you say. Of course they do. But, as I say, no one in their *right* mind would want to do it, would they?

No.

The situation was definitely a serious one. And something had to be done.

Jimmy felt very sorry for himself, as he sat with his feet in a bowl of mustard water, his nose in hot steaming vapours, and his head wrapped in warm towels.

"Oooooh," he moaned from under the towels, "I've got a really nasty head cold, as described in *Biggles Has A Really Nasty Head Cold*."

Yob was thumbing through a large medieval encyclopedia. He had recently obtained a degree in Medieval Studies through the Open University. It would not, however, help him in his struggle to find employment, as he had already eaten the certificate. He was also on his third bowl of Friars Balsam. He couldn't see why so many people raved about it. He thought it tasted horrible.

"Ah! Here we are," said Yob, having found what he was looking for. "Nostrialus Snottius — more commonly called the Common Cold. 'Nostrialus Snottius — more commonly called the Common Cold is . . . incurable'."

"Bloomin' marvellous, isn't it!" exclaimed Jimmy. "They can send a man to Dover and back, but they can't cure the common cold!" Just then his form-mates, led by an anxious Mad, piled into his cramped shelter.

"Grim news, oh Battle of Britain chum!" she told him.

"The Head's a computer!" PC told him.

"Who's now mega-powerful after an overdose of electricity!" Doughnut told him.

Jimmy held up a sickly hand. "Let's get this straight," he said. "The Head doesn't work off gas then?"

This is going to be more difficult than we thought, thought Mandy.

"What's a computer?" asked Jimmy.

In Santa's Grotto, which had been transformed for the purpose by the addition of rows of desks, the parents sat staring at their exam papers.

"Right," commanded the Head. "You have seventeen years to answer sections 1 to 8 of the paper. There will then be a ten-minute break, after which you will have 24 years for the final part of the paper, and not a second more. Turn over."

Mrs Quiff 'n Airy turned over. Then she turned back. Then she turned the paper over. She would clearly be there for many, many years to come.

In the shelter, Jimmy shook the cold from his head.

"It seems to me that we should take a leaf out of *Biggles Beats The Mad Computer Head*! In it, the goodies use a skilful ruse to gain access to the computer."

"What skilful ruse?" asked Mandy, who was all ears. No, sorry. It's William who's all ears, isn't it?

"A suicidal diversionary attack," said Jimmy.

"Splendid!" enthused Mad. "Who's qualified to lead the suicidal diversion?"

"Yeah," scoffed Nick. "Who's stupid enough?" He felt a dozen pairs of eyes boring into him.

"What? Me? You're joking!" Nick complained.

"But Nick," Mandy pleaded, "if you don't do something brave and totally stupid, we'll never free our parents!"

"Look no further for a foolhardy Fuhrer!" said William who, you will have noticed, had been silent up until now. "One will do it!"

"Oh, Willy!" Madeline gushed, with love in her eyes.

The others just cheered.

The heat was unbearable in the Christmas jungle, as Commander Windsor led his weary and battle-scarred troops through the dense mass of harmful hanging streamers, deadly dangling milk bottle tops, and fearsome fairy-lights. He had been pushing his men for days, but still they seemed no nearer to their goal, the lair of the Mad Computer Head. They must go there to save the hostages. But they were dropping on their feet. He must let them rest. It was a risk. But it was a calculated one.

"Right, fall out for five minutes!" He barked the order at his men, without meeting their eyes.

"You can't keep pushing the men like this," his trusty second-in-command, Sergeant Mad, confided in him as they snatched the much-needed rest.

"You don't think I like it, do you?" he rounded on her, savagely. "But there's a job to be done, and by golly one is going to do it!"

Not all his men were made of such stuff.

"I can't go on!" raved Private Knuckle. "I can't take it anymore! I've got to get out of this tropical Christmas jungle." He had recently seen action in another galaxy, and had not been the same since.

"That man there! Sit down!" barked the ruthless Commander.

"You can't make me! I've had enough I tell you!"

"You take one step to desert . . . " warned the steely-eyed Commander Windsor, as he drew his Christmas cracker from its holster, "and I'll cracker you like the dog you are!"

This time their eyes met. The cold gaze of the Commander. The panicking exhausted eyes of the lesser man. It was Private Knuckle who cracked, and fell sobbing to the jungle's parquet floor. His "oppo", the newly-made-up Corporal Quiff knelt to comfort him. They went back a long way. Quiff looked his Commanding Officer full in the eye.

"You're a hard man," he said, steadily. "I hope you're proud of what you've done today."

Further conflict was prevented by the arrival of Jimmy, known to his mates (and there were many) as "Jimmy".

"I've been scouting ahead, as described in *Biggles Scouts Ahead*," he reported, after a salute. "We've done it! The Head's study is just round the corner!"

"Commander Windsor could not believe his ears. "We've . . . done it?" he asked, in a daze.

Good news always travels fastest. And this was no exception. "We've done it! We've done it!" chorused the other ranks.

"Thanks to you," said Sergeant Mad, softly, "You never gave up hope, did you?"

"Very nearly, Mad. Very nearly." Oh. If only she knew how close it had been.

"Right, you lot," he barked down the line. "Cut the cackle! Let's get this job done!"

And the column moved forward, with a spring in its step, and a whistled carol on its lips.

They had always known that the final battle, when it came, would be tough. It could go one of two ways: they could win, or they could lose.

Windsor knew that he and his men were the diversion. He also knew that some of them might not come back. That was the price you paid for freedom.

Outside the Head's study window, the main Task Force — PC, Doughnut and Mandy — were awaiting the signal. The signal was the sound of the battle. That would tell them that the brave boys had got through.

"They're late," said PC, on edge.

"They can't have got through!" Doughnut was fearing the worst. Then it came.

"Listen," whispered Mandy. They listened. They heard.

The battle was on.

Christmas tree decorations, even thrown very hard, are no match for bolts of pure energy. The

Task Force were badly outclassed. But they had Grit and Determination on their side.

The Head fought off attack after attack. But they came back for more.

"Revolting pupils! Do you think you can overcome me with mere force! I'll totally obliterate you! I will sentence you to eternal detention!" And he cackled. Even Jimmy's playing of the bagpipes didn't bother him.

"Let him have it, PC!" Harry yelled over the battle's roar. "De-programme him!"

"Ha! Ha! Do you think a tadpole brain like her could de-programme a mega-brain like me?"

"He's right," admitted PC.

The situation seemed hopeless. But Doughnut had an idea. "I've got an idea!" he said. I told you he had. "Who was it who gave Mr Grunter the Astro-Physics and Gardening teacher a nervous breakdown?" Doughnut said.

All eyes turned to Mandy. "I only told him about my collection of drip-mats and double-glazing leaflets." Mandy pointed out, with typical modesty.

"Yes," continued Doughnut. "But for fourteen hours!" Doughnut then whispered to Mandy: "Mandy, approach the Head and engage him in small talk . . . "

And she did.

She talked. And talked. And talked. And talked.

She talked about how long she'd been coming to the school, to the exact second, and how many bricks it had taken to build the school. She talked of removable roof-racks, self-assembly stereo units, relative absorption of different brands of paper hankies, the value of the double knot when tying shoe laces, Panda versus Pelican crossings . . . She gave no quarter.

And then she went for the Big Kill: shoe dye.

It worked.

The Head exploded.

SAFE AND SOUND

The Carol Concert went ahead as planned. The parents were greatly relieved, as it meant that they didn't have to complete the exam, which had proved more difficult than even they could have imagined. The first problem for most of them had been the first question: Name. But, after much pencil chewing, staring into space and a little bit of cheating, they had that one done. And at least they'd made a start, although Mr Knuckle-Tattoo wasn't convinced that they'd got it right. I mean, they couldn't all be called The Duchess of York, could they? Still, they were all in it together, and they must help each other. Mrs Doughnut got the answer to the one about "Why did Archimedes shout 'Eureka!' and jump out of the bath?"

It's obvious!" she explained. "The water was too hot." Two answers down, and only 7,985,432 to go!

As Jimmy broke down the door, as described in *Biggles Breaks Down The Door,* Mrs Quiff 'n Airy was tackling the question about Phythagorus' Theorem, but she couldn't quite remember whether only some of the squares were on a hippopotamus, or all of them. She also couldn't remember where playing the triangle came into it. So Jimmy's arrival was, for her at least, very welcome. Mr Knuckle-Tattoo, on the other hand, was getting into his stride, and seriously considered applying for the Open University."

"That'd be great," he explained to his wife, who was less sure. "I mean, cus all the lessons are on the telly, so if you get bored you can switch over and watch *Emmerdale Farm.*"

However, this was not to be. The Carol Concert beckoned, and soon they were in the hall, in the bosom of their respective familes, and in fine voice.

And, as they sang, the pupils of Palace Hill reflected:

The past Term had been an eventful one.

Harry had won and lost Peanut.

William had lost Peanut, but found Madeline. She was now "By Royal Appointment".

Doughnut and Mandy had realised that beauty is not skin deep. They too had found each other.

Bonnie and Clyde had found that money wasn't everything, but it was better than most things.

They had all, in their way, learned some of the lessons that life had to teach. This was part of the pain and the pleasure of growing up.

And here they all were. The parents and the pupils. Safe and sound once more. Side by side in blessed harmony, all bound in one common celebration. Love and warmth in their hearts, music on their lips . . .

"I don't believe it! He's done it again!" It was Mrs Knuckle-Tattoo who broke the mood. Mr Knuckle-Tattoo had broken something else, just seconds earlier. And he wasn't wearing leather trousers!

EPILOGUE

Clyde had had a hard morning. It had been his painful duty to make several of the staff redundant. It may have seemed tough, but they knew the rules when they joined the organisation. Compulsory early retirement for older staff. And these were all older staff. I mean, one of them was practically thirty! It was harsh, but Clyde hadn't got where he was today by being soft.

One of them was taking it very badly. Sobbing uncontrollably. He decided that he must do something.

He sold her a handkerchief.

As he rung the money into the till, he reflected: Bonnie and he had come a long way since they first stood, scrubbed and shaking, in front of the forbidding gates of Palace Hill. That now seemed millions of years away. Certainly millions of pounds away. And here they were, among the ten richest people in the country, wined and dined by nobility. Why, they'd even been on *Wogan* (but not *Bob Says Opportunity Knocks*). They would have to buy the BBC. There was nothing else for it.

Flushed with success, Clyde joined Bonnie at the front doors of this, their latest and largest Megastore. They had an important appointment with the Prime Minister. They were going to do something for their country. They were going to lend it some money. As Clyde arrived, their personal limousine drew up. Bonnie and Clyde stepped into the back. Clyde picked up the internal telephone and spoke sharply to the driver.

"Number Ten, Downing Street, Knuckle. And be quick about it."

"Yes, Guv."

"And don't call me Guv."

"No, Guv. Sorry, Guv."

And so the limousine glided away, past the magnificent frontage of their latest business venture, with its windows crammed with beautiful, expensive things. Past the army of security men who guarded the beautiful expensive things. Finally, past the twenty foot statue, the symbol of their business empire — a magnificent, hand-carved Blue Dolphin.